THE
BONESETTER'S
DAUGHTER

Amy Tan

*spark notes

© 2020 SparkNotes LLC
This 2020 edition printed for SparkNotes LLC by Sterling Publishing Co., Inc.

ISBN 978-1-4114-8028-5

Distributed in Canada by Sterling Publishing Co., Inc.
c/o Canadian Manda Group, 664 Annette Street
Toronto, Ontario M6S 2C8, Canada
Distributed in the United Kingdom by GMC Distribution Services
Castle Place, 166 High Street, Lewes, East Sussex BN7 1XU, England
Distributed in Australia by NewSouth Books
University of New South Wales, Sydney, NSW 2052, Australia

For information about custom editions, special sales, and premium and corporate
purchases, please contact Sterling Special Sales at 800-805-5489
or specialsales@sterlingpublishing.com.

Manufactured in Canada

Lot #:
2 4 6 8 10 9 7 5 3 1
09/20

sparknotes.com
sterlingpublishing.com

Please email content@sparknotes.com to report any errors.

CONTENTS

CONTEXT

Аmy Tan's fiction, including *The Bonesetter's Daughter*, often focuses on the Chinese-American experience and the bond between mothers and daughters. Tan's interest in these themes comes from the circumstances of her own life. She was born in Oakland, California, in 1952. Her parents immigrated from China, and Tan's experience growing up as the American child of Chinese parents shaped her identity and her writing. Tan has openly spoken about her difficult relationship with her mother, and the complicated bond between mothers and daughters is a major theme in many of her novels. Tan's mother kept significant aspects of her own past secret for years and only revealed them once Tan was grown. For example, Tan eventually learned that her mother had been previously married and had children from this marriage, whom she left behind in China. As an adult, Tan traveled to China with her mother to meet the half-sisters she had never known. The idea that mothers have secret pasts unknown to their daughters is an important theme in Tan's fiction, appearing in *The Joy Luck Club* and *The Bonesetter's Daughter*, two of Tan's acclaimed novels.

Details drawn from Tan's life and family history appear in *The Bonesetter's Daughter*. Tan's maternal grandmother committed suicide when Tan's mother, Daisy, was young, and throughout Tan's childhood and adolescence, Daisy often threatened to commit suicide herself. Because of the trauma she experienced in China, Daisy was regularly preoccupied with the idea of curses and ill fate. Around the time Tan began writing *The Bonesetter's Daughter*, Daisy was diagnosed with Alzheimer's, and she died before the novel was completed. When she was a college student, Tan's roommate was murdered, and due to the trauma of identifying the body, Tan temporarily lost the ability to speak. For years afterward, she would lose the ability to speak on the anniversary of the murder. All of these details appear in the novel in some form.

Tan also interweaves historical events into the plot of *The Bonesetter's Daughter*. In 1927, a team of scientists began a formal excavation of a site in Zhoukoudian, China. They discovered fossilized remains of a previously unknown subspecies of the prehistoric species *Homo erectus* (a species of archaic human). This discovery attracted worldwide attention, and excavations yielded approximately 200 fossils from at least 40 different specimens. The subspecies became known as Peking Man and was widely celebrated as an important archaeological discovery that could shed important light on the history of human evolution. In 1937, the excavations ceased due to the outbreak of war between China and Japan. The fossils were first stored at Union Medical College in Peking (modern-day Beijing) in hopes that excavation could resume after the end of the war, but as hostilities increased, it became too dangerous to leave the fossils in Peking. In 1941, the fossils were packed up to be shipped to the United States but vanished en route. They have still never been located, and the disappearance remains unexplained.

While the excavation of the Peking Man represents a specific historical event, the broader scope of twentieth-century Chinese history creates another important context for the *The Bonesetter's Daughter*. In the novel, LuLing is born in 1916, when her mother is approximately twenty years old, which means that Precious Auntie is born some time at the very end of the nineteenth century, when China is still under imperial rule. By this time, however, the Emperor had lost significant power. In 1912, a few years before LuLing's birth, the Republic of China is established. By 1927, civil war breaks out in China between the Republican government and the Communist Party of China. This conflict is reflected in the fates of LuLing and GaoLing's brothers, who either choose to fight on the side of the Communists or are conscripted into the opposing army. Civil war continues to rage until the outbreak of hostilities with Japan in 1937. The Second Sino-Japanese War (which eventually becomes part of World War II) is usually thought to originate with the Marco Polo Bridge Incident, which Tan references in her novel. Other effects of the war—such as Americans in China being considered prisoners of war after 1941—also appear in the novel. Tan includes this historical content in *The Bonesetter's Daughter*, but she mainly focuses on the ways in which these historical events affect the lives of individuals, especially women.

Plot Overview

Ruth Young is a Chinese-American woman in her forties who lives in San Francisco and works as a ghostwriter. Ruth has a stable life but is sometimes troubled by doubts about her relationship with her boyfriend, Art. She often feels overwhelmed by the stress of managing her career and her family life, which includes acting as a stepmother to Art's two adolescent daughters. Ruth has a close but ambivalent relationship with her elderly mother, LuLing. LuLing raised Ruth as a widowed single mother, and the two of them often fought, especially since LuLing has always had a bad temper and a history of depression. Ruth is distressed to find that her mother is showing signs of forgetfulness and confusion. When LuLing is diagnosed with dementia, Ruth becomes eager to learn about her mother's past. Years before, LuLing gave Ruth a document in which she wrote down some of her life story, but, since the document is written in Chinese, Ruth struggled to read it and has made little effort to persevere. After LuLing's diagnosis, Ruth finds the remainder of the document and decides to have it professionally translated. While she waits for the translation to be completed, Ruth moves in with her mother to help care for her.

The handwritten document tells the story of LuLing's life. She was born in 1916 in a small town in China, not far from the city of Peking. LuLing was born into the Liu family, a prosperous family of ink-makers, and grew up in an extended family unit with her sister GaoLing, brothers, parents, aunts, uncles, and cousins. The most important person in LuLing's life, however, was her nursemaid, Precious Auntie. Precious Auntie was a mysterious woman who had severe scarring and was unable to speak. LuLing communicated with her through writing and other means and acted as a translator for the rest of the family. In the document, LuLing reveals events from Precious Auntie's life that took place before she was born. It is later revealed that LuLing knows this information because of a document Precious Auntie wrote for her.

Precious Auntie was raised by a man who worked as a bone-setter and healer, using both traditional and modern medicine. Because she was the only surviving child and her father was a widower, Precious Auntie grew up well-educated, independent, and

3

accustomed to thinking for herself. She was also very beautiful, and her beauty eventually attracted proposals from both a man named Chang, who worked as a coffin maker, and Baby Uncle, the youngest son of the Liu family. Precious Auntie accepted the proposal from Baby Uncle because she was in love with him, and the couple began to have a sexual relationship before they were married. On the day of the wedding, Baby Uncle followed tradition and escorted Precious Auntie and her father to his house along with gifts from the bride's family. These gifts included the "dragon bones" that were found in mountain caves nearby and used in healing rituals. The traveling party was attacked by men who appeared to be bandits. Precious Auntie's father was killed in the attack, and all the valuables were stolen. Baby Uncle was killed immediately after the attack when he vowed revenge and his horse kicked him. Precious Auntie was convinced that Chang orchestrated the attack as revenge for her rejection of him.

Precious Auntie was taken to the Liu house to recover from her grief, but in despair, she tried to kill herself by drinking burning ink. This left her scarred and permanently unable to speak. When it became clear that she was pregnant with Baby Uncle's child, the Liu family decided to cover up the scandal of an illegitimate birth. The baby, LuLing, was adopted by Baby Uncle's eldest brother and his wife and passed off as their own child. Precious Auntie was allowed to stay and care for her child, but no one ever told LuLing that her nursemaid was actually her true mother. LuLing and Precious Auntie were very close, but as LuLing became a teenager, their relationship became more strained. LuLing began to see Precious Auntie as a lower-ranking woman whom she did not want to listen to, and she also became more ambitious about her own future.

When LuLing was almost fifteen, she was summoned to meet with the family of a prospective husband. LuLing later learned that she was being considered as a wife for one of Chang's sons. She was happy about this because the marriage would mean becoming wealthy. However, Precious Auntie had always insisted that Chang was responsible for the death of Baby Uncle, and she forbade the marriage. LuLing ignored her and did not read the document Precious Auntie gave her. In despair, Precious Auntie killed herself, and after she died, LuLing read the document and finally learned that Precious Auntie was her true mother. The family now believed that LuLing was associated with bad luck, so they sent her to an orphanage run by American missionaries. While living there,

LuLing became a teacher and married a man she loved. Eventually, GaoLing joined LuLing at the orphanage, running away from her own unhappy marriage to Chang's son.

When World War II broke out, the situation became dangerous. LuLing's husband was killed, and GaoLing and LuLing moved to Peking together. When the war ended, GaoLing had the opportunity to immigrate to America, so she left and promised to sponsor LuLing to join her. While she waited, LuLing worked hard to earn money while living in Hong Kong. Eventually, GaoLing met two brothers, Edmund and Edwin Young, who were both looking for wives. LuLing went to America, married the elder brother, and gave birth to Ruth. However, her husband died when Ruth was a baby, so she had to raise Ruth by herself, while GaoLing lived a much more prosperous life with her husband and two children. LuLing has always been filled with regret and grief about what happened to Precious Auntie and even believes that she can communicate with her spirit.

Once Ruth reads the document and learns the true story of her mother's life, she becomes much more compassionate toward her. With Art's help, Ruth is able to move LuLing into an assisted living home, which LuLing enjoys. Ruth finally tracks down Precious Auntie's real name and feels a much deeper connection to her family history. She now has a happier relationship with Art and begins to write a story in her own voice for the first time.

CHARACTER LIST

Ruth Young The protagonist of the novel. Ruth is a middle-aged woman who has a generally happy life but is often left wondering why she does not feel entirely satisfied. Ruth focuses on making everyone around her happy, but she is disconnected from her own ambitions and desires. She carries a legacy of pain from a difficult relationship with her mother and also has an ambivalent relationship with her identity as a Chinese-American person.

LuLing Young The mother of Ruth Young and one of the novel's main characters. LuLing is an elderly woman who is often stubborn, cranky, and melodramatic. She is set in her ways and thinks that she has all the right answers. Over time, LuLing emerges as a more sympathetic character because some of her behavior is explained by her diagnosis of dementia, and her handwritten document reveals that she has lived through many tragic events.

Precious Auntie The mother of LuLing and the grandmother of Ruth. Precious Auntie is an intelligent and charismatic woman who experiences many tragic losses, including the losses of her father and first love. The impact of her grief leads her to attempt suicide twice, and she is terribly scarred and unable to speak. Precious Auntie is resilient and willing to make many sacrifices to care for her daughter, but she is also held back by shame and loss.

GaoLing (Auntie Gal) Young Ostensibly the younger sister of LuLing, but actually LuLing's cousin. GaoLing has a comfortable life as the matriarch of a prosperous multi-generational Chinese-American family. Unlike LuLing, she is not haunted by her past life in China.

However, she also has secrets and lived for years with a new husband without disclosing that she already had a husband in China.

Art Ruth's partner. Art is a sensitive man and caring father. He loves Ruth but also takes her for granted. Art upholds an American outlook and value system, and this sometimes makes it hard for him to relate to Ruth's Chinese-influenced upbringing.

Kai Jing Pan The first husband of LuLing. Kai Jing is a gentle and thoughtful young man. He is always loving toward LuLing and treats her with respect. Even though he and LuLing only spend a short time together, he gives her a lifetime of loving memories.

Edwin Young The second husband of LuLing. LuLing does not reveal much about Edwin's personality, but he had a bright future when he died tragically young. LuLing often states her belief that Edwin was smarter and would have been more successful than his brother.

Dory Art's daughter. Ruth acts as a stepmother to Dory, and they have a stable, if not particularly close, relationship.

Fia Art's other daughter. Ruth acts as a stepmother to Fia, and they have a stable, if not particularly close, relationship.

Wendy Ruth's longtime friend. She knows Ruth well but also has trouble understanding Ruth's choices because she had a different upbringing.

Edmund Young GaoLing's husband and Ruth's uncle. Edmund was always considered to have as much potential as his elder brother, but once Edwin died, Edmund takes on a leadership role in the family. He is a quiet and mild-mannered man.

Mother   The woman LuLing grows up believing to be her
                mother and the wife of the eldest Liu brother. Mother
                is a superstitious and unforgiving woman. She is
                never happy that Precious Auntie remains part of the
                family, and she blames Precious Auntie for all the
                misfortunes the family encounters. She is very shrewd
                and intelligent and good at handling a crisis.

Chang   A prosperous coffin maker from the same town as the
                Liu family. Chang is a cruel and unscrupulous man
                who hurts and exploits others to get what he wants.
                His legacy of abuse leads to financial instability and
                drug addiction within his family.

Fu Nan Chang Chang's son and GaoLing's first husband. Fu Nan
                is a lazy and cowardly man whose life revolves around
                his opium addiction. While he is a greedy bully, he
                lacks the intelligence or motivation to be a real threat
                to anyone.

Ruth Grutoff The American missionary who runs the orphanage
                where LuLing ends up living. She is a kind and
                brave woman who tries to provide good care for the
                children.

Mr. Tang   An elderly Chinese-American scholar who translates
                LuLing's manuscript so that Ruth can read it. He is
                intelligent and compassionate, and he is so moved by
                the story of LuLing's life that he falls in love with her.

Teacher Pan   LuLing's first father-in-law. He is a well-educated and
                caring man who is loving and nurturing toward both
                his son and LuLing. He treats LuLing as a daughter
                even after the death of his son.

Billy   Ruth's cousin

Sally   Ruth's cousin

ANALYSIS OF MAJOR CHARACTERS

RUTH YOUNG

Ruth is the protagonist of *The Bonesetter's Daughter*, and the plot is driven by her struggle to find a sense of connection with her mother and greater confidence in her own identity. Ruth often feels frustrated and embarrassed by her mother because she has always wanted to blend in and receive the approval of others. When Ruth thinks about her childhood and adolescence, she dwells on the ways that LuLing failed her. Ruth can recognize that her mother worked very hard to give her economic stability and a good education, but she cannot feel true gratitude because she is preoccupied with longing for affection and emotional intimacy, which she does not believe she experienced. Ruth often compares her life to the lives of those around her, and this leads her to feel like she is missing out on things. At the same time, she lacks the agency to make any changes that could improve her life or relationships.

As the novel progresses, Ruth experiences personal growth when she asserts herself and takes action. The fear of losing her mother eventually motivates Ruth to get LuLing's life story manuscript professionally translated and to move in with LuLing for several months. Before that, Ruth had been stuck in a rut, passively waiting for something to come along and change the nature of her relationships with her mother and partner, Art. Ruth's choice to move in with LuLing gives her additional perspective and understanding in both relationships. She gains many new insights into LuLing's history, and she develops better communication with Art. This new understanding empowers Ruth to live the life she wants. She develops the confidence to assert herself in her relationship with Art, and she takes steps toward writing her own book instead of revising the stories of others. Once Ruth learns about the courage of the generations of women who came before her, she begins to see herself as more resilient and capable. Ruth stops focusing on self-pity and regret and starts trying to live her life in a way that would make her strong mother and grandmother proud.

LuLing Young

LuLing is motivated by conflicting desires to keep her past a secret but also atone for the guilt she feels about it. When LuLing moves to America, she wants to leave behind her unhappy memories and sense that she is cursed. She believes that she can have a fresh start, but her dreams of a happy new life are shattered when her second husband dies early in their marriage. LuLing has now lost two husbands, and she is left to raise a child alone with few economic resources. These circumstances cause LuLing to believe that she is being punished for her failure to love and respect Precious Auntie. She blames herself for her mother's death and for her inability to give her mother's bones a safe resting place. LuLing wants to keep her past behind, but she is tormented by regrets every day. This inner conflict explains the erratic behavior Ruth observes growing up, which often hurts her. LuLing hides the truth of her past life but also gives clues to the reason for her obsession with the past when she tries to communicate with the spirit of Precious Auntie.

LuLing is only able to find peace once her daughter fully knows her history. Ruth never explicitly tells her mother that she has read the manuscript, but her behavior toward LuLing becomes gentler and more compassionate. LuLing senses this shift in her daughter and becomes calmer and more agreeable. She even reaches out to spontaneously apologize to Ruth for the ways she hurt her as a child. Even though LuLing no longer has the cognitive ability to fully understand or remember what happened, she can understand the shift between herself and her daughter on an emotional level. In addition to a better relationship with Ruth, LuLing has the first truly intimate relationship she has had in years with Mr. Tang. He knows LuLing's past, and he admires and loves her because of who she is. LuLing has lived with shame and a sense of unworthiness for so long that it is profoundly healing for her to have a companion who shows no judgment or disappointment.

Precious Auntie

Precious Auntie is resilient and strong, but her strength is a liability for her. Precious Auntie receives an unconventional upbringing where she is treated more like a son than a daughter. While the novel generally focuses on the bond between mothers and daughters, Precious Auntie grows up motherless and identifies with her father instead. She thinks of herself as "the bonesetter's daughter." Because of her childhood, Precious Auntie mistakenly believes that she can make her own decisions about her future. She does not understand the depth of the consequences of rejecting Chang's marriage proposal until it is too late. Precious Auntie's first suicide attempt is a reaction to the loss of Baby Uncle and her father, but her terrible grief also represents a moment in which she confronts what it means to be a woman. She would rather die than live with the powerlessness of the female experience. Precious Auntie's terrible scars symbolize her transition from being outspoken and independent to being literally silenced. To cover up the scandal of having a baby with Baby Uncle out of wedlock, Precious Auntie now must live as a household servant and lose any status or respect she might previously have held.

Precious Auntie can withstand anything except her daughter's rejection. She is willing to live a humble life of secrets because, within this life, she can still find joy in her daughter's company, even if LuLing does not know her true identity. With LuLing's wedding to Chang's son imminent, Precious Auntie takes a desperate gamble. Because of her own loyalty to family, she assumes that once LuLing knows the truth about their relationship, she will obey Precious Auntie. Precious Auntie mistakenly believes that LuLing does learn the truth and still rejects her, and she cannot bear this knowledge. Precious Auntie's suicide appears to be at odds with her otherwise resilient character, but it reflects just how much she longs to be truly seen and beloved. She finally offers honesty about herself and cannot bear to be rejected by the one person she has left. Still, even Precious Auntie's death reflects her need to protect her child. By killing herself, she believes she gains a superstitious power to scare off the Chang family and protect LuLing, even at the ultimate cost to herself.

THEMES, MOTIFS & SYMBOLS

THEMES

Themes are the fundamental and often universal ideas explored in a literary work.

MOTHER-DAUGHTER RELATIONSHIPS

Throughout *The Bonesetter's Daughter*, the examples of mother-daughter relationships prove that love can coexist with conflict and that familial patterns will perpetually repeat. Both Ruth and LuLing grow up raised by mothers who have sacrificed a lot to care for them, but they lack knowledge of their mother's histories and consequently fail to appreciate their mother's sacrifices. As they reach adolescence, Ruth and LuLing both grow increasingly rebellious and lash out against their mothers because they feel ashamed of them. The frustration and resentment they feel toward their mothers does not negate their love, and both daughters later look back and regret their behavior. In fact, the conflict both generations of mothers and daughters experience is rooted in their desire to protect one another. They carry deep love but experience similar conflict because generational trauma is passed down and experienced by each mother and daughter pair.

RESILIENCE

Characters in the novel—especially women—who are systematically denied power become resourceful in other ways. The female characters in the novel experience violence and abuse, a lack of economic opportunities, and an inability to make decisions about their own lives, such as whom to marry. Even Ruth, growing up in contemporary California, is still at risk of sexual violence. The women, living in different time periods and different regions, have a shared experience of being stripped of their power, and they become resilient and resourceful. LuLing and GaoLing survive tragic events, but they eventually travel to America and build new lives for themselves. Even though Precious Auntie kills herself, she passes down her intelligence and skills to her daughter. Even Mother shows great

strength and shrewdness when it seems like the Liu family fortune
has been lost.

SECRECY

In the novel, withholding truth leads to lingering, persistent trauma.
Precious Auntie thinks she is protecting her daughter and giving
her a better future by hiding her true identity as LuLing's mother.
LuLing takes the same approach and thinks that she will spare
Ruth the pain of generations before by not revealing her history.
However, for both women, withholding the truth from their daughters fractures their relationships. LuLing's lack of knowledge leads
to Precious Auntie's suicide, which then haunts LuLing for the rest
of her life. Still, LuLing keeps important secrets and only narrowly
avoids Ruth living her entire life without knowing the truth about
her mother. Ruth and LuLing have a tense relationship because
Ruth cannot realize how difficult LuLing's life has been. Contrary
to LuLing's fears, once Ruth knows the truth about her, she is much
more patient and loving with her mother.

MOTIFS

*Motifs are recurring structures, contrasts, or literary
devices that can help to develop and inform the text's
major themes.*

BONES

Bones represent the importance of a connection to the past. Bones
are typically left behind after someone or something dies, and thus
they show that few things vanish entirely. Everyone leaves behind a
trace, and what is left needs to be treated with respect and reverence.
The fossilized bones that are initially thought to be "dragon bones"
or "oracle bones" turn out to be the bones of the Peking Man, a
prehistoric human. These bones reflect a profound human desire to
understand one's history to better understand oneself. While much
of the story relies on Ruth's personal journey to understanding her
immediate family ancestors, humanity as a whole needs a connection to its ancestors. Bones, of course, also exist within living bodies
and are part of the ancestral profession of Precious Auntie's family.
Bones are central to the childhood accident where Ruth breaks her

arm. In this sense, bones represent resilience and healing, since a broken bone is painful but can heal if it is cared for properly.

GHOSTS

The motif of ghosts reveals the challenges of establishing an independent identity. Ruth works as a ghostwriter because she does not feel confident in writing in her own voice or telling her own story. She eclipses her identity behind the identity of another author because she feels safer that way. Her work as a ghostwriter is, in fact, foreshadowed by her childhood, when LuLing believed that she could communicate with the ghost of Precious Auntie. LuLing's belief that Precious Auntie continues to be an active presence in her life shows that she has a hard time separating her own identity from a longing for her lost mother. LuLing's loss was particularly traumatic because she only learned Precious Auntie's identity after the suicide and never had the chance to know her mother as her mother. Even though LuLing has a daughter of her own and has moved to a new country, her obsession with Precious Auntie's ghost shows her inability to truly establish a new identity for herself.

SUICIDE

Suicide is a motif that reoccurs across three generations of characters, showing how trauma is passed down and self-harming behaviors can be inherited. Precious Auntie first tries to commit suicide while pregnant with LuLing and then succeeds in killing herself fifteen years later. LuLing regularly threatens to commit suicide and makes a serious attempt when Ruth is a teenager. Ruth has been haunted by ideas of suicide throughout her life, and she considers it as an option when she mistakenly believes that she is pregnant. Precious Auntie's first suicide attempt is rooted in her lack of control over her fate, and her death ignites a legacy of trauma that continues on with both her daughter and granddaughter. LuLing is at an impressionable age when she has the horrific experience of finding her mother's body, and her response to future pain is usually to resort to threats of suicide. The moment when she lost her mother was also when LuLing truly understood their bond, so when she threatens suicide later in life, she is also, ultimately, trying to find a way to connect with Ruth in a meaningful way.

Symbols

*Symbols are objects, characters, figures, or colors used
to represent abstract ideas or concepts.*

The Pearl Necklace

The pearl necklace symbolizes the deceit and lack of transparency in the relationship between Ruth and LuLing. Ruth buys an inexpensive necklace of fake pearls as a gift for her mother but is embarrassed when LuLing mistakenly believes the necklace to be valuable. Ruth has never told her mother the truth but remains tormented by shame and embarrassment because of the falsehood. The necklace thus reflects how Ruth has never learned to tell the truth to her mother, presumably because LuLing has never modeled honesty herself. The value of the necklace is relatively unimportant, but the fact that Ruth finds it impossible to speak the truth shows just how difficult honesty is for the two women. The necklace also symbolizes how once a lie or secret takes hold, it gains power. If Ruth had immediately told the truth, her shame would have been contained, but after years of silence, telling the truth seems impossible and her shame intensifies.

Precious Auntie's Scars

Precious Auntie's scars symbolize the secret she keeps and the shame she feels about the tragedy she believes she caused. Although she was once a beautiful young woman, her suicide attempt leaves Precious Auntie grotesquely scarred and unable to speak. Her whole identity changes, and she loses her connection to her previous life as the bonesetter's daughter, when she was confident and outspoken. She can never own her new identity as LuLing's mother, so her scars are the physical manifestation of her inability to speak the truth. Precious Auntie sees herself as the cause of her father and fiancé's deaths and wears her scars as a reminder of her guilt. Because she bears the marks of the tragedy on her skin, her guilt and regret are advertised to the world. Precious Auntie's self-loathing and shame are implicitly passed on to her daughter, who will blame herself for her mother's death.

THE ORACLE BONE

The oracle bone symbolizes Precious Auntie's connection to her birth family and her pride in her lineage. After Precious Auntie begins living as a nursemaid, she loses her social status as the daughter of a respected artisan. Because she cannot claim her daughter as her own, the official lineage of her family will die with her. However, though she cannot openly claim LuLing as part of the bonesetter's line, by giving her the oracle bone, Precious Auntie ensures that LuLing will always have a connection to her mother's family. It is eventually revealed that the oracle bone is a valuable ancient artifact. Even though Precious Auntie and her family may not have fully understood what the bone was, they had an inherent sense of its value, and Precious Auntie reveals her love for LuLing and her pride in her family history by giving her the bone.

SYMBOLS

SUMMARY & ANALYSIS

TRUTH & PART ONE: CHAPTER ONE

SUMMARY: TRUTH

LuLing Liu Young opens the novel by introducing herself, her two husbands, and her daughter, Ruth Luyi Young. When LuLing was six years old, Precious Auntie showed her a piece of paper with her family name written on it. Precious Auntie was scarred and disfigured and communicated with LuLing through a mixture of writing, sign language, and gestures. Precious Auntie was very close to LuLing and took care of her every day. On the morning that Precious Auntie shared her family name with LuLing, she took the young girl to pray and burned the paper with the name written on it. Now, LuLing is frustrated by her inability to remember the name. She invokes Precious Auntie's help, revealing that she is Precious Auntie's daughter, and that this family name is therefore her own lost name as well.

SUMMARY: CHAPTER ONE

The narrative shifts to the voice of an anonymous narrator who explains that every August, Ruth Young loses her voice. This strange occurrence started when Ruth moved in with her partner, Art, and now reoccurs on every anniversary. To cope, Ruth voluntarily stops speaking for approximately one week and has come to enjoy this period of silence. It has now been nine years since she and Art moved in together, and Ruth spends this anniversary at Lake Tahoe with Art and his two young daughters, Dory and Fia. The trip does not go as well as Ruth hoped, and they return to their home in San Francisco in a state of tension. Late that night, Ruth finds herself unable to sleep or relax. In the clutter of her desk, she finds a document written in Chinese. Her mother, LuLing, gave her this document a few years before, explaining that she had been writing down the story of her life. Ruth has a limited ability to read Chinese, so it takes her a long time to make sense of the document, and she has not gotten far. She has gradually drifted away from the project, even though the first few lines alone already revealed information she had not previously known about her mother. Now feeling guilty,

Ruth decides that she will hire someone to translate the document for her.

The next morning, Ruth contends with the cramped space of her apartment. She ponders her similarities to her mother now that she is in her mid-forties and is constantly stressed due to juggling her work and caring for her stepdaughters. She receives a call from her best friend, Wendy, who is eager to share her news that her elderly mother has married a much younger personal trainer. After the phone call, Ruth takes the girls to their ice-skating lessons. Ruth reflects on how she often feels ambivalent about her interactions with them and with Art, even though most of her friends believe she has a perfect relationship. Ruth and Art met almost ten years ago, when Ruth and Wendy enrolled in a yoga class. When Art showed interest in her, Ruth misinterpreted it because she thought he was gay. They began to meet regularly. Art worked in linguistics research, and Ruth was an editor and ghostwriter. Ruth discussed her previous serious relationship, which ended when she and her partner drifted apart and he took a job in New York without consulting her. Art shared that he was divorced with two young daughters, and Ruth realized that she was mistaken in thinking he was gay.

Back in the present day, Ruth continues with her domestic tasks and calls Wendy again to further discuss their mothers. Their discussion reminds Ruth that she is supposed to take her mother to a doctor's appointment that afternoon. She is going to accompany her mother to the check-up because she has noticed small changes in her mother's behavior and wants to see if there is reason to be alarmed.

ANALYSIS: TRUTH AND CHAPTER ONE

The opening section introduces the three main female characters and hints at some of the similarities between them. LuLing has precise memories of events from her childhood, but some details, such as her family name, escape her. While LuLing cannot recollect the name that Precious Auntie shared with her, her memory implies that the name carries a kind of sacred power with it. Precious Auntie wrote the name down so that LuLing could create a visual memory of it, and this action becomes more significant when readers later learn that Precious Auntie's ability to write was a prized skill that she passed down to LuLing at a time when it was not common for women to read and write. By watching Precious Auntie write down the name of her family, LuLing is introduced to a bit of Precious

Auntie's past and the pride she takes in her lineage. The fact that LuLing cannot recall the name implies that there has been some sort of fracturing or loss in her relationship to Precious Auntie.

LuLing introduces herself through a web of relationships and links to her past. Almost as soon as she states her name, she begins to describe the relationships and people she is intertwined with. LuLing does not see herself in an individualistic way; instead she defines herself according to her relationship with others. She feels a deep connection to her past, demonstrated as she articulates a sense of longing for the lost memory of the name and for an intimacy with Precious Auntie. LuLing's concluding comment that she is Precious Auntie's daughter introduces an element of suspense and mystery into the plot because it is unclear exactly why she refers to this woman as "auntie" and yet calls herself her daughter. Precious Auntie's scarring also hints that some sinister event took place in her past.

Ruth's narrative is completely different in its setting and worldview, creating a sense of distance between the lives and experiences of LuLing and Ruth. Ruth lives the life of a modern American woman, which comes with both opportunities and pressures. She has a thriving career, but this requires her to spend many hours working and trying to meet the needs of others. She has a distinctively modern romantic relationship in which she lives with a divorced man she is not married to and spends time nurturing his daughters without having biological children of her own. Despite the appearance of freedom, there are hints that Ruth's life is not entirely happy. Her annual silence seems to be connected in some way to her relationship with Art and suggests that she feels powerless or voiceless in the relationship. Although Art behaves as a generally loving partner, he also occasionally takes Ruth for granted and assumes that she will manage many of their domestic affairs even though she has her own demanding career. Though Ruth's narrative is starkly different from her mother's, Ruth's recurring voice loss parallels Precious Auntie's inability to speak and suggests that there might be commonalities between the two women.

Unlike LuLing, Ruth focuses on her present rather than the past. It has been a few years since she received the document from LuLing, and she has not made much of an effort to figure out what it says. Ruth's limited ability to read Chinese reflects her disconnection and disengagement from her cultural heritage. Her career revolves around her ability to communicate expertly in English, implying that her values and interests are tied to contemporary life in America, not to any sense of connection to the past. Ruth also assumes that her mother's life story could not possibly be very interesting because she does not prioritize learning more about it. Additionally, Ruth's inability to read the manuscript parallels LuLing's inability to remember the name she read all those years ago. Both women have lost a connection to something that holds clues about their mothers.

PART ONE: CHAPTERS TWO & THREE

SUMMARY: CHAPTER TWO

> *In an odd way, she now thought, her mother was the one who had taught her to become a book doctor. Ruth had to make life better by revising it.*
> (See QUOTATIONS, *p. 51*)

Ruth goes grocery shopping and reflects on her childhood filled with frugality and practical necessity. Back at home, she tries to focus on her work even though she feels unmotivated. Over the past fifteen years, she has contributed to almost thirty-five books, mostly in the realm of self-help, wellness, and New Age philosophy. She sometimes feels sad that she does not get much credit or recognition for her work, even though her mother takes pride in her career. Ruth does not like conflict or confrontation, partially because her mother often gets in arguments and fights. She has also often been embarrassed by her mother's poor English skills. She finds LuLing's difficulty with English surprising because her mother's sister, GaoLing, came to America at the same time but speaks much better English. Because household tasks take longer than expected, Ruth is running late when she goes to pick up her mother. LuLing is healthy for a 77-year-old woman and does not go to the doctor frequently, but Ruth is concerned that she has recently grown forgetful. However, it is hard for Ruth to gauge changes in LuLing's moods because LuLing has been angry and depressed for all of Ruth's life and has regularly threatened to commit suicide.

LuLing lives in a modest home with a tenant who rents the down-stairs unit from her. Ruth is concerned when she arrives because the tenant comes out and complains about LuLing behaving strangely and abusively toward her.

LuLing is a skilled calligrapher and painter. When Ruth was a child, LuLing worked as a teacher's aide and supplemented her income by doing Chinese calligraphy on signage for local businesses. LuLing tried to teach Ruth to write in Chinese and told Ruth about how she was taught to write by a woman named Precious Auntie, who had cared for her as a child.

Ruth now observes her mother showing signs of confusion: she has misplaced her purse and cannot remember the correct time of the appointment at the doctor's office. Ruth reflects on the complex relationship between her mother and her aunt. The two women are only one year apart in age and married a pair of brothers after immigrating to America. LuLing married Edwin Young, who was the elder brother and a medical student, while GaoLing married Edmund, who attended dental school. It seemed that LuLing had the brighter future ahead, but Edwin was killed in a hit-and-run accident when Ruth was only two years old. Edmund has become respected and wealthy, especially since he inherited most of his father's money, and Ruth and LuLing received only a small inheritance. LuLing set this money aside and eventually combined it with years of saving to purchase the house where she still lives. During Ruth's childhood, LuLing often expressed her frustration that she ended up with so little money and lived a life that was much more difficult than the life of her sister.

SUMMARY: CHAPTER THREE

Ruth and LuLing arrive at the doctor's office, which specializes in providing services to Chinese patients. LuLing's forgetfulness leads Ruth to repeat herself about the death of her beloved cat, even though she shared this news with LuLing months ago. The doctor reports that LuLing is in excellent health but becomes concerned when LuLing evades basic questions he asks her. As the conversation continues, LuLing becomes more confused and erratic in her responses, and eventually Ruth speaks with the doctor privately, admitting that she has noticed signs of mental confusion in her mother for months. The doctor suggests running additional tests and returning for a follow-up appointment in a month since several conditions could be causing LuLing's confusion. That night, LuLing has dinner with Ruth, Art, and the girls, but the dinner is unpleasant because LuLing keeps scolding Ruth about the girls' behavior, and the girls are irritated by her presence.

As a child, Ruth changed schools frequently, causing her to be friendless and lonely. One day, when Ruth was six, her mother embarrassed her by scolding her on the playground in front of other children. Ruth defiantly threw herself down the slide and broke her arm. To Ruth's surprise, the accident made the other children much nicer to her, and it also caused her mother to treat her with more kindness. Awed by how much better her life had become, Ruth stopped speaking. She believed that if she spoke, things would go back to normal. Her mother encouraged her to write rather than speak, and this also gave Ruth positive attention from the other children at school. Ruth was surprised by how her mother asked for her opinion and perspective in a way that she had never done before. One day, Ruth realized that her mother believed Ruth could communicate with the spirit of Precious Auntie. LuLing became very eager for Ruth to ask the ghost questions about whether she forgave LuLing and whether the curse had been lifted, but Ruth didn't understand what her mother was talking about. LuLing promised to one day return to China and find the missing bones of the spirit.

In her apartment, Ruth considers phoning Miriam, Art's ex-wife, to ask if the girls can join the family reunion she is organizing. Ruth hesitates and thinks about the intimacy she still senses between Art and Miriam. Their closeness is confusing because Ruth is much more reserved and does not like to ask Art for a lot of details about his past life.

ANALYSIS: CHAPTERS TWO & THREE

This section reveals more about LuLing's character from Ruth's perspective. Ruth is obviously not an impartial observer; she has complex yet ambivalent feelings about her mother. As a single mother and child, LuLing and Ruth spent virtually all of their time together and were each other's primary sources of companionship, which made Ruth both dependent and uncomfortable. LuLing's limited English abilities added another layer of complexity to their dynamic. Even as a young child, Ruth always had a certain level of responsibility and was required to help her mother. Ruth's need to act as a translator parallels how LuLing was required to interpret for Precious Auntie, who was unable to communicate with anyone else because of her injuries. Throughout her life, Ruth has had a challenging relationship with her mother because of LuLing's intense and erratic personality.

LuLing's history provides some explanation for why she has become a bitter woman. Although she had the presence and support of her sister, GaoLing, immigrating to California meant leaving behind all of her friends and family and an entire way of life. LuLing's hopes were then crushed by the abrupt death of her second husband. She lost the possibility of enjoying an economically comfortable life from her husband's career as a physician and position as the Young family's eldest son and heir. LuLing and GaoLing's choice of prospective husbands forms an interesting contrast with Ruth's approach to romantic relationships. While Ruth is secure in her own career and chooses Art because she enjoys his company, her mother and aunt viewed their choice of husbands as the way to attain economic security. LuLing's plan failed, but GaoLing's succeeded, and this has created a rift between the women.

Ruth's personal and professional life revolves around ensuring that others get their needs met. While she takes pride in her career, she does not get public credit for the work she does, and she does not have the agency to communicate her own ideas. Ruth struggles to fully express herself and articulate her true ambitions and desires, meaning she experiences a metaphorical silence (in addition to the physical silence she experiences upon losing her voice each year). The other silent character in the novel, Precious Auntie, is silent because of terrible scars, and while Ruth is not physically scarred, the parallel between the two women suggests that Ruth carries some sort of psychological wound within her. When she talks with her friend Wendy, Ruth is astonished by the intimacy and open communication that seems to exist between other couples. Ruth's earliest model of emotional closeness was her mother, and the communication barrier between them meant Ruth has never learned what it is like to truly share herself with someone.

Ruth's professional role parallels her personal role as a de facto stepmother and caregiver. She must shoulder many personal burdens and responsibilities, but she does not get the recognition or rewards that others do. Especially as LuLing's behavior has become more erratic, Ruth steps into more of a caregiving role, reversing the earlier parent-child dynamic. Moreover, Ruth has to juggle competing demands between people who are important to her. There exists both generational and cultural tension between LuLing and Art's daughters. The young girls cannot relate to LuLing, do not feel any bond with her, and do not feel an obligation to respect her. LuLing has much different ideas about how children should be raised, and she is surprised to see her daughter participating in a family life that is very different from the one she understands. Ruth is often frustrated because she has a responsibility to both LuLing and Art's daughters, but they don't feel obligated to listen to her in return.

Ruth's childhood memory of breaking her arm reveals how underlying power dynamics in her relationship with LuLing first became established. As the child of an immigrant parent, Ruth wanted to fit in, so she was often embarrassed by LuLing. Breaking her arm symbolically connected her to Precious Auntie and to the bone healers in her maternal ancestry. At the time, however, all Ruth knows is that both her mother and her peers treat her with more kindness when they believe that she is hurt. Ruth paradoxically gains power by becoming vulnerable: when she stops speaking, people nurture and care for her. The incident teaches her that bravery is dangerous, but being quiet and uncomplaining is rewarded. Although Ruth may not see the connection as a child, readers understand how this accident likely shaped her subsequent character. Even as a woman in her forties, Ruth tries to be docile, unobtrusive, and agreeable. She still goes through periods of silence, which may now reflect an unconscious desire for greater tenderness or attentiveness from Art, in the same way that silence earned her mother's affection when she was a child.

The bone-breaking incident also sparks LuLing's belief that her daughter can commune with the spirit of Precious Auntie. Ruth's writing on the tray of sand evokes memories of how LuLing and Precious Auntie once communicated and makes it seem possible that a voice is being channeled through Ruth and into the words she writes. The lack of communication between mother and daughter is what makes this whole mistake possible. Ruth has no idea what her mother is talking about when her mother begins to rant about curses, bones, ghosts, and unburied bodies. In Ruth's mind, this confirms that LuLing is either mentally unstable, hopelessly superstitious, or both. She is unable to recognize the truth in LuLing's words because she does not understand her mother's history.

PART ONE: CHAPTERS FOUR–SIX

SUMMARY: CHAPTER FOUR
The narrative resumes a month later, at the time of the Full Moon Festival. Ruth is organizing a dinner for her extended family and includes Art's parents, Miriam and her new husband, and Miriam's

two young boys. Ruth is not excited about this arrangement, because Art's parents have always preferred Miriam and continue to have a close relationship with her. Ruth's cousins, Billy and Sally, come with their respective spouses and children. Although there are a few tense moments, the dinner goes well, and Ruth is moved to see her family and friends gathered together. Ruth presents her mother and aunt with a photo of the two of them as young girls but is surprised when LuLing refers to Precious Auntie as her mother instead of the woman Ruth has known as her grandmother. Ruth is confused. She knows Precious Auntie as the nursemaid who cared for her mother, endowed her with many superstitious beliefs, and killed herself when LuLing was fourteen. She cannot understand why LuLing is now referring to Precious Auntie as her mother and worries that this is another symptom of LuLing's mental confusion. This worry worsens when LuLing gives Ruth a pearl necklace that Ruth had actually given her as a gift years ago. Ruth remembers the necklace because she has always felt bad about it. Though the pearls are fake, LuLing mistakenly assumed the necklace was expensive and has taken a lot of pride in it. Now she makes a show of giving it to Ruth, while Ruth quietly burns with shame.

SUMMARY: CHAPTER FIVE

When Ruth and LuLing attend the follow-up doctor's appointment, LuLing is diagnosed with dementia. However, LuLing does not understand the diagnosis or what it means. Over the next three months, Ruth has her mother join her and Art every night for dinner. She observes LuLing acting angrier and more erratic, which makes everyone around her uncomfortable. Ruth and Art have a vacation to Hawaii planned, but Ruth feels like she cannot leave her mother. Art suggests that Ruth hire a house cleaner and a nurse to help LuLing, but Ruth feels frustrated that he focuses only on the pragmatic details of the situation and not on her emotions. She feels less and less connected to Art and worries about the fact that the two of them have never gotten married.

Ruth lies to her mother, telling her the house cleaning is free. Most of the housekeepers quit quickly, and Ruth ends up spending a lot of time at LuLing's house helping in their wake. Finally, Art leaves for Hawaii alone. Ruth is grateful for the time to gather herself; her work and health are suffering because of the amount of time she devotes to caring for her mother. She is scheduled to pick up LuLing for dinner, but LuLing does not answer her calls and is not at her house when Ruth arrives. Ruth learns from the downstairs tenant that LuLing wandered off wearing only pajamas. Alarmed, Ruth phones the police but is embarrassed when LuLing returns almost immediately. Ruth is concerned about her mother's deteriorating condition and calls Auntie Gal, who offers to have LuLing come and stay with her.

SUMMARY: CHAPTER SIX

> She recalled that when her younger self stood on this same beach for the first time, she had thought the sand looked like a gigantic writing surface. The slate was clean, inviting, open to possibilities. And at that moment of her life, she had a new determination, a fierce hope.

(See QUOTATIONS, p. 51)

Ruth walks to the beach and reflects on a traumatic experience from her childhood. When Ruth was eleven, she and LuLing moved from Oakland to Berkeley and rented a bungalow from a young couple named Dottie and Lance Rogers, who lived in a larger house on the same property. At this time, Ruth was often frustrated with her mother, especially living in cramped quarters, and annoyed by her mother's frequent requests that she contact the spirit of Precious Auntie. Ruth became fascinated with observing the relationship between Dottie and Lance, and also developed a crush on Lance. She was delighted when Lance and Dottie invited her to watch *The Wizard of Oz* on their new color television. LuLing was hesitant, but Ruth manipulated a supposed message from Precious Auntie in order to make it seem that Precious Auntie approved of the activity. LuLing allowed Ruth to go, and while at the house, Ruth used the bathroom immediately after Lance and accidentally got some of his urine on her when she sat on the toilet.

A few days later, Ruth attended a health class, which provided some limited information about puberty, menstruation, and how babies are conceived. When Wendy later told her that pregnancy results from a man urinating inside a woman, Ruth believed her. Realizing that she had been in contact with Lance's urine, she became terrified that she was pregnant. She considered killing herself but eventually confided in Wendy. Wendy told Dottie that Ruth was pregnant with Lance's baby. Ruth was astonished that Dottie was protective of her and angry with Lance. She heard the couple fighting later that night, and Lance drove away. The next day, Dottie asked her some questions, preparing to go to the police and charge Lance with rape. However, as Ruth explained the details, Dottie realized her mistake with horror. Shortly thereafter, Lance returned to the house, and Dottie moved out. When she next crossed paths with him, Lance invited Ruth into the house. At first, he acted friendly, but he eventually became aggressive and tried to sexually assault her. Ruth got away but could no longer bear to live near Lance. Pretending to be the spirit of Precious Auntie, she wrote a message urging LuLing to move to San Francisco. LuLing trusted this message, and mother and daughter moved to San Francisco, where they lived ever since.

ANALYSIS: CHAPTERS FOUR–SIX

The New Moon Festival dinner highlights how Ruth struggles to straddle different value systems and the consequences of her lack of insight into LuLing's past. Ruth is conspicuously the only one among her cousins who is not married and does not have children, and this worries her. Ruth also has to find a way to integrate Art's non-Chinese family into the traditions of her own. Some of them are more open-minded than others, but many are guarded. Other than her mother, Ruth does not spend much time with other Chinese-Americans. Her partner and close friends are all Caucasian. While this might reflect Ruth's identity as part of a multicultural society, it also highlights another way in which she feels disconnected from her mother. LuLing's identity is rooted in her Chinese heritage, but her daughter does not have the same sense of belonging.

Because Ruth has not read the manuscript LuLing gave her years ago, she sees LuLing's comments about Precious Auntie as possible signs of dementia. Even the short initial section of the manuscript refers to LuLing as the daughter of Precious Auntie, but Ruth has made no effort to fully translate the document. Thus, she is confused when LuLing comments at dinner that Precious Auntie is her mother. The information she misses by refusing to engage with her mother's life story foreshadows how readers will later learn that LuLing once refused to read the manuscript Precious Auntie gave her and remained ignorant, with terrible results. This incident also shows the consequences of long-kept secrets. Because LuLing has kept her mother's identity a secret for so long, no one believes or understands her when she openly starts to speak the truth.

LuLing's deteriorating condition highlights the fragility of Art and Ruth's relationship and their different values. The relationship has largely worked due to Ruth's independence and willingness to put the needs of Art's family ahead of her own. With the increasing burden of caring for her mother, Ruth can no longer attend to domestic responsibilities in the same way. If anything, she now needs Art to help her, but he acts unable to do so. Because Ruth has not previously shared her emotions and needs with Art, he cannot anticipate what is making this situation challenging for her. He tries to focus on tangible actions that he thinks could save Ruth time, but he doesn't realize the complex layers of emotions and guilt that she feels. What Ruth is really mourning is the belief that LuLing is someone she can depend on.

Ruth's stress about her mother's deteriorating condition brings up memories of past stresses, including a foundational trauma that marked her transition from childhood to adolescence. LuLing did not provide her daughter with any sort of sexual health information. Additionally, Ruth's school gave her obscure and incomplete sexual education, which only rendered her more confused. This lack of transparent information about how her body works left Ruth vulnerable to misinformation. Ruth's mistaken belief that she might be pregnant with Lance's child also shows the toxic impact of secrecy. Ruth absorbed the message from her mother that shame should be kept to oneself, and by the time Dottie got the full story from Ruth, the damage has already been done to Dottie and Lance's relationship. Ruth seriously considered suicide when she thought she was pregnant, but she was still not able to talk with her mother about what had happened, demonstrating the depth of their commitment to secrecy.

While Ruth was never able to communicate openly about what happened, she secretly asserted agency over the situation in order to get what she needed. After Lance tried to sexually assault her, Ruth needed to protect herself and move far away from Lance. To ensure this result, she played to LuLing's greatest weakness: her reliance on Precious Auntie's "ghost." LuLing believed so strongly that the spirit of Precious Auntie gave Ruth valuable information that she obeyed Ruth's words without question. Ironically, LuLing was more attentive to the requests and needs of a ghost than those of her own daughter. This was partially because LuLing was so driven by guilt that she was desperate to atone in any way she could. The reliance on the supposed voice of Precious Auntie also hints that LuLing wrestled with fearfulness and confusion about how to provide a good life for her daughter. If she were more confident in herself and her choices, she would not have clung so desperately to instructions from a spirit. Ruth learned that she cannot get her needs met by asking openly. Her inability to tell LuLing what happened to her foreshadows how, decades later, she finds it so hard to explain her grief and sadness to Art.

PART ONE: CHAPTER SEVEN & PART TWO: HEART

SUMMARY: CHAPTER SEVEN

In the present day, Ruth returns to LuLing's home and cleans up. Sifting through items, Ruth remembers growing up as a rebellious teenager. She wanted to carve out a life for herself that was very different from what she saw her mother experiencing. Ruth wrote about many of these feelings in her diary, though she suspected that LuLing would find and read it. When Ruth was fifteen, she and her mother were at a particularly antagonistic point in their relationship. After they had a fight about Ruth smoking cigarettes, Ruth wrote in her diary that she hated her mother and wished that LuLing would kill herself. The next day, Ruth came home to find out from her Auntie Gal that LuLing had fallen from a window. Horrified, Ruth realized that her mother must have read the diary and tried to kill herself. As Ruth helped her mother recover from her injuries, she tried to be as kind and docile as possible. For Ruth's sixteenth birthday, she received a Chinese Bible and a beautiful jade ring that belonged to LuLing. However, it turned out that LuLing was only promising her the ring for the future. LuLing and Ruth continued fighting often, and Ruth eventually abandoned the diary in a hiding place in the apartment.

As Ruth looks through the apartment, she finds a long document written in Chinese and realizes that there is much more of the manuscript than the few pages LuLing gave her years ago. Worried about the limited time she may have remaining with her mother, Ruth makes a series of decisions. She decides to get the entire document professionally translated so that she can learn what her mother has been writing about. She also wants to speak with Auntie Gal to see what she knows about LuLing's past, and then she wants to spend more quality time with her mother, gradually asking questions about her past. To achieve this, Ruth plans to move in with LuLing.

SUMMARY: HEART

> *In this way, Precious Auntie taught me to be naughty, just like her. She taught me to be curious, just like her. She taught me to be spoiled. And because I was all these things, she could not teach me to be a better daughter, though, in the end, she tried to change my faults.*
>
> *(See* QUOTATIONS, *p. 51)*

LuLing narrates the history of her life. She was born in a small town in China, not far from Beijing (known at the time as Peking). Her family—the Liu family—had lived in the town for generations and made a comfortable living as inkstick makers. They had a shop in Peking that sold the ink, and the male members of the family spent much of their time dealing with that aspect of the business, while the physical manufacturing of the ink was largely handled by the women in the large family compound in the town of Immortal Heart. As a child, LuLing was surrounded by family: her parents, her sister GaoLing, several brothers, her great-grandmother, and aunts, uncles, and cousins. Her father was the eldest son of the Liu family, giving him a position of power and authority. He had three younger brothers: Big Uncle and Little Uncle, who each had wives and children, and Baby Uncle, the youngest. LuLing abruptly reveals that Baby Uncle was actually her father and goes on to give the back story of her real parents, who are not the people she refers to as Mother and Father.

Precious Auntie grew up in a nearby town, where it was common practice to gather bones from local mountain caves and sell them to fortune-tellers and healers. Precious Auntie's father came from a long line of bonesetters who treated individuals with injuries and collected bones from mountain caves to use in their medical treatments. When LuLing was a child, Precious Auntie took her to a hidden cave and showed her where "dragon bones" could be found. Because her mother and siblings died when she was young, Precious Auntie grew up much more independent and better educated than was typical for a young girl at the time. However, this unusual upbringing made her less desirable as a wife in the eyes of many, even though she was very beautiful. LuLing pauses to explain that she learned these details about Precious Auntie's life because the latter wrote down pages about her history and gave them to LuLing.

One day, when Precious Auntie was nineteen years old, her father treated an infant who was the son of a man named Chang, the local coffin maker. Chang seemed malevolent, and there was an implication that he might have been abusing his wife and children. Later that same day, the bonesetter also treated a young man, Baby Uncle. Both Chang and Baby Uncle became interested in Precious Auntie, and a short time later, Chang asked the bonesetter for permission to take Precious Auntie as his second wife. She refused, and the bonesetter made a polite excuse to Chang. However, only a few days later, Precious Auntie accepted the proposal from Baby Uncle, which sent Chang into a jealous rage. Although frightened by his threats, Precious Auntie focused on her hopes for a happy future. Precious Auntie and Baby Uncle began a sexual relationship before their marriage.

On the day of the wedding, Baby Uncle followed tradition and escorted Precious Auntie and her father to his house along with gifts from the bride's family. These gifts included the "dragon bones" that were found in mountain caves nearby and used in healing rituals. The traveling party was attacked by men who appeared to be bandits. Precious Auntie's father was killed in the attack, and all the valuables were stolen. Baby Uncle was killed immediately after the attack when he vowed revenge and his horse kicked him. Precious Auntie was convinced that Chang orchestrated the attack as revenge for her rejection of him.

Precious Auntie was taken to the Liu house to recover from her grief, but in despair, she tried to kill herself by drinking burning ink. This left her scarred and permanently unable to speak. When it became clear that she was pregnant with Baby Uncle's child, the Liu family decided to cover up the scandal of an illegitimate birth. The baby, LuLing, was adopted by Baby Uncle's eldest brother and his wife and passed off as their own child. Precious Auntie was allowed to stay and care for her child, but no one ever told LuLing that her nursemaid was actually her true mother.

ANALYSIS: CHAPTER SEVEN & HEART

The climax of Ruth and LuLing's turbulent relationship shows just how capable they are of wounding one another. Although she is initially a very docile and meek child, Ruth becomes a defiant adolescent after the move to San Francisco. She loses faith in LuLing's ability to protect her after the incident with Lance, and she also realizes that she can manipulate LuLing, which causes her to lose respect for her mother. Developmentally, as Ruth moves into her teenage years, it also becomes more important for her to develop an identity distinct from her mother's values. Ruth's increasing defiance leads to more conflict between mother and daughter. Because Ruth knows so little about her mother's past, she does not understand why LuLing is so threatened by her increasingly willful behavior. A seemingly trivial fight about Ruth smoking cigarettes leads to Ruth lashing out and LuLing attempting suicide. In keeping with the important theme of written messages, Ruth's message of anger and loathing is communicated in the message she writes in her diary. Similarly, throughout the novel, notions of public and private blur around written documents. Precious Auntie and LuLing both write documents that are intended to be shared with their daughters but are otherwise deeply intimate and personal. Ruth keeps a diary that is ostensibly private but which both she and LuLing know that LuLing is reading.

One tragic aspect of LuLing's suicide attempt is that it does not actually bring mother and daughter together. The two women do not develop a more open or emotionally intimate relationship. In fact, after a time, Ruth goes back to her rebellious ways. The lack of narrative between the time of the suicide attempt (when Ruth is sixteen) and the present-day narrative thirty years later indicates that there has been a sort of deadlock in their relationship. Things have not gotten worse, but they also have not gotten better. In the present day, facing the possibility that her time with LuLing is running out, Ruth finally becomes more proactive about learning more about her mother. Up until this point, she has largely remained passive and simply wished for a different type of relationship with LuLing without doing anything about it.

Now that Ruth has taken on the more responsible care-giving role in the relationship with LuLing, she also becomes more active. The simple step of hiring a translator so that she can understand her mother's life story represents a choice to meet LuLing halfway. Rather than being frustrated by the gap in their language, Ruth chooses to accept circumstances for what they are and work within them. This acceptance of reality represents the first step toward accepting LuLing for who she is. This decision showcases a step for Ruth away from being a petulant child who blames her mother for strange behavior to a calm and curious adult who wants to learn about the experience of someone else. It is only when she fears that she might lose the opportunity to learn about LuLing that Ruth is motivated to act. While she has often felt taken for granted and resentful, she has, in turn, taken her mother for granted.

The narrative of LuLing's life begins with a significant account of the life of her mother, Precious Auntie, which highlights how foundational Precious Auntie is in LuLing's story. The story of Precious Auntie's life is important to make sense of the secrets LuLing has carried with her, but it also speaks to the symbolic connection across generations. LuLing cannot tell the story of who she is without explaining who her mother is because their identities are inseparably intertwined. LuLing has access to context and knowledge about their family history that Ruth has never had. However, LuLing did not always have this clarity and insight. She grew up under the shadow of secrecy, not knowing that Precious Auntie was her mother or how Precious Auntie received her scars. Still, LuLing's early childhood passed in a relatively happy fashion. She had closeness with one special person, similar to the bond between LuLing and Ruth, and also had the support of a large extended family.

The histories of LuLing's parents reflect themes that resonate in her own life and Ruth's. The Liu family's profession as ink-makers reflects LuLing's interest in calligraphy and painting and Ruth's eventual career as a writer. The bonesetters of Precious Auntie's family represent an ability to heal and uncover secrets. Broken bones are painful, but they also have the capacity to mend. Likewise, Ruth and LuLing realize over time that fractured and unhappy relationships can be mended if both parties proceed with care for one another. Precious Auntie's father learned his profession from his father, and his father before him, and he possessed valuable knowledge that could only be passed down through a family lineage. His life represents the continuity of family tradition and cultural connection that is fractured when Precious Auntie is forced to keep a secret from her own daughter. The title *The Bonesetter's Daughter* refers to Precious Auntie specifically, but also symbolically to all of her female descendants who are part of the same lineage.

Precious Auntie is a woman ahead of her time. She is independent, well-educated, and capable. She follows her heart when she chooses to marry Baby Uncle and when she begins a sexual relationship with him before their marriage. Even though she lived decades earlier, Precious Auntie is more sexually aware and liberated than LuLing or even Ruth. However, the world in which Precious Auntie lives is still patriarchal and violent, and she is punished for trying to think for herself and follow her heart. The roadside death of Baby Uncle in a sudden accident mirrors the sudden hit-and-run death of LuLing's second husband decades later. Precious Auntie's suicide attempt reflects the pattern of suicide that will echo across the generations. She is so consumed by guilt and grief that she tries to kill herself through gruesome means. Her physical scars and silencing mean that she is left with a lifelong reminder of her loss.

Precious Auntie's resilience and courage are what allow LuLing to have the life she does. Her tragic loss figuratively as well as literally silences Precious Auntie, but she manages to move forward for herself and her daughter. At the time that LuLing is born, an illegitimate child was considered shameful, so the Liu family made a collective decision to protect both her and the family honor. Precious Auntie consents even though it means that she will have to live a lie. She will also lose her social position and be treated as though she is a servant, while the other wives enjoy the comfortable lives that easily could have been hers. This experience of social downfall after the death of her husband-to-be is parallel to what LuLing will later experience when she is widowed. Even though Precious Auntie has endured many losses and has to live a hard life, LuLing does not remember her mother as a bitter woman. Instead, Precious Auntie wanted to give her daughter as many happy memories as possible. She is happy to devote her entire life to LuLing even if it can never be revealed what their true relationship is.

Part Two: Change, Ghost & Destiny

Summary: Change

After growing up with a happy childhood, LuLing's life changes in 1929, when she is fourteen years old. A group of scientists and archaeologists become very interested in excavating the nearby caves where bones are discovered. Rumors swirl that there may be human bones in the caves, and eventually information comes to light about the excavation of the Peking Man. Any bones from the caves become very valuable, but Precious Auntie refuses to sell the bones she has kept from her father's medical practice. Instead, she returns them to the hidden cave. This decision frustrates LuLing because she dreams of the family becoming rich and famous. As LuLing grows older, she has become confused about why Mother seems to favor GaoLing over her, even though LuLing is older. Precious Auntie's low social status also makes LuLing somewhat ashamed of her, and she some-times gets tired of her role acting as Precious Auntie's interpreter.

Soon, the village hears news that Chang sold some dragon bones to the scientists that turned out to be human bones, and he has received a lot of money. Most of the Liu family is interested in this news since they respect Chang. Precious Auntie, however, has always insisted that Chang was responsible for the attack on her wedding day, but no one believes her. She is furious now because she thinks that the dragon bones Chang sold are the ones that were stolen during the attack years earlier. Precious Auntie's behavior increasingly irritates Mother, and she seems to be considering send-ing the nursemaid away. A short time later, Great Granny dies, and when Chang comes to the Liu house to deliver the coffin, LuLing accidentally mentions that Precious Auntie hid bones in a cave but didn't tell anyone the location of the cave.

A few months after Great Granny's death, a distant relation who dabbles in matchmaking, reaches out to indicate that a local fam-ily with many sons has taken an interest in LuLing, who is now of marriageable age. They would like her to come to Peking so that she can "accidentally" meet the family and the match can be consid-ered without the pressure of a formal meeting. There is a discussion about whether Precious Auntie should go with her, and LuLing does not advocate for her nursemaid because she is afraid of Precious Auntie embarrassing her and hurting her chances of the match. In the days leading up to LuLing's departure, the two of them fight more and more since Precious Auntie is strongly opposed to the young girl going to Peking alone. LuLing leaves on bad terms but is dazzled by her experience in Peking. At the meeting, she meets her prospective mother-in-law, who turns out to be Mrs. Chang. Mrs. Chang appears interested in having LuLing as a wife for one of her sons. LuLing is excited by the prospect of marrying into a wealthy and well-regarded family, even though she still has not met her prospective husband. She returns from Peking feeling self-satisfied. When LuLing returns to her home, she immediately tells Precious Auntie that there is a good chance she will marry one of the Chang sons. Precious Auntie is horrified and tries to forbid it, but LuLing refuses to listen.

SUMMARY: GHOST

LuLing receives an offer to join the Chang family as a daughter-in-law, and her family is eager to accept. Her relationship with

Precious Auntie remains tense, but a few days before LuLing is supposed to leave for her new home, Precious Auntie gives her a written manuscript describing the history of her life. LuLing, however, refuses to read it. She lies and tells Precious Auntie that she has read it but that she is still determined to marry into the Chang family. The next morning, the family (including LuLing) finds Precious Auntie's body. She has killed herself. The Chang family receives a letter stating that Precious Auntie's ghost will haunt them if they go ahead with LuLing's marriage. Mother is furious and has Precious Auntie's body thrown into the ravine behind the house rather than buried. Finally, LuLing reads the manuscript and learns that Precious Auntie was her true mother. She goes to the ravine to search but cannot find the body. Her marriage is called off, and the only person in the family who now treats her with kindness is GaoLing.

Two weeks later, the Liu family receives tragic news that their shop in Peking has burned down, taking much of their inventory with it. Worse still, they may have to pay damages to the owners of the nearby shops that also burned. They believe that these unfortunate events resulted from the anger of Precious Auntie's ghost. As they wait to hear what the damages will be, they hire a local exorcist to deal with the ghost, and he claims he has sealed it up. The family's fortunes change quickly for the better, which makes them even more convinced that the ghost was responsible for their misfortune. Afraid of the bad luck that LuLing might bring to them, they announce that they are sending her to an orphanage.

Summary: Destiny

LuLing arrives at an orphanage run by Christian missionaries who were not expecting her. However, they are impressed by her ability to read and write elegant calligraphy, skills that Precious Auntie taught her. They allow her to stay so that she can be the assistant to Teacher Pan, who is responsible for teaching the older students. There are about seventy girls and babies at the orphanage, most of whom are illegitimate and some of whom are disabled. The two Americans who run the orphanage are Miss Grutoff and Miss Towler, and they have a staff of former students to help them. A portion of the orphanage is also rented out to scientists who are involved in the Peking Man excavation. Teacher Pan has a son named Kai Jing who works as a geologist and sometimes helps his father at the orphanage. The girls also sometimes travel to the excavation site to help with simple tasks. LuLing treasures the manuscript Precious Auntie gave her, and one day she discovers that the manuscript's cover contains one of the dragon bones and a photograph of Precious Auntie from before she was scarred.

After LuLing has been at the orphanage for two years, she receives a letter from GaoLing. It has taken GaoLing that long to track down LuLing's location since the family refused to tell her where LuLing was sent. GaoLing married into the Chang family in place of LuLing, as part of a business deal where the Chang family lent the Liu family money to rebuild the shop. Now, both the Chang and Liu families have serious financial problems, and many members of the Chang family are also addicted to opium. GaoLing leads an unhappy life, but LuLing's life has recently transformed: she has fallen in love with Kai Jing.

ANALYSIS: GHOST, CHANGE & DESTINY

As LuLing matures into a teenager, her previously happy relationship with Precious Auntie becomes much more tense and fraught. LuLing's behavior is similar to the defiant arrogance Ruth will display decades later, which implies that regardless of time and place, there are some universal realities about mother–daughter relationships that play out time and time again. Because LuLing hides her history from her own daughter, they are doomed to repeat it. The way in which LuLing's rebellion manifests reflects the cultural values of the time. LuLing becomes increasingly interested in money and status because these are values that are prized by the Liu family. Because she has lost her connection to her bonesetter heritage, LuLing has also lost her connection to the values of integrity and tradition. She cannot understand why Precious Auntie will not sell the valuable bone or condone her marriage into the Chang family. While LuLing's self-centered approach is partially a function of her being a spoiled teenager, it also results from her ignorance. Because she does not know the full story of who she is or what Precious Auntie's history has been, she cannot have compassion for her. This ignorance mirrors the way Ruth has often been frustrated and impatient with LuLing without knowing the context of her suffering.

While the winds of change impact the relationship between LuLing and Precious Auntie, forces of modernity also invade the traditional lifestyle of the village. In 1927, a team of Chinese and Western scientists excavate a site near Peking after discovering what appeared to be fossilized remains of a previously unknown subspecies of the prehistoric species *Homo erectus* (a species of archaic human). This discovery attracted worldwide attention, and excavations yielded approximately 200 human fossils from at least forty different specimens. The subspecies became known as the Peking Man. Tan uses the backdrop of this historical event in her novel, presenting it in the context of a local family. The presence of bones in the caves where the fossils were eventually found had been part of local lore for generations, but the local people did not have the archaeological or scientific knowledge to identify these bones as the remains of early humans. Precious Auntie's father and fore-fathers, however, had long recognized a special power and value in these bones, calling them "dragon bones." As forces of contempo-rary capitalism and colonialism encroach, the stakes for decisions like LuLing's marriage become even more heightened.

LuLing's stubborn defiance produces tragic consequences that will haunt her for the rest of her life. First, she refuses to engage with Precious Auntie's fears and forebodings about the Chang fam-ily. Precious Auntie is not just being spiteful; she is committed to keeping her daughter safe. Precious Auntie knows of the history of domestic violence within the Chang family and fears what might lie ahead for LuLing. However, LuLing is not interested in Precious Auntie's fears because she assumes she herself knows best and thinks of Precious Auntie as superstitious and out of touch. LuLing feels disdain for Precious Auntie's mistrust of the Chang family in a way that parallels the disdain Ruth will feel for LuLing's devotion to Precious Auntie's spirit. LuLing cannot be bothered to read the manuscript Precious Auntie gives her and lies when she says she has read it. While Ruth fails her own mother in similar ways, she is, at least, transparent about delaying reading the manuscript.

Because Precious Auntie mistakenly believes that LuLing rejects her even after learning that they are mother and daughter, she is unable to bear her grief any longer. She has lived her whole life in the hope that she might someday tell the truth to her daugh-ter, and now that her revelation has failed, she has no reason to live. Thus, LuLing lives with the tragedy Ruth narrowly avoids: she learns the truth of her mother's story only after her mother is dead and gone. LuLing finds her mother's body and then the corpse is thrown into a ravine. In a culture where veneration and commemo-ration of deceased family members was an important cultural and spiritual practice, the erasure of Precious Auntie's body is a particularly devastating blow. Additionally, in light of this lack of burial, the loss of Precious Auntie's name is even more devastating. Other than LuLing's memories and a photograph, there is no evidence that Precious Auntie ever lived.

Like her mother, LuLing ends up ostracized by conservative social forces. Suicide was considered unlucky and shameful, and the Liu family does not want the circumstances of Precious Auntie's death to be revealed. This incident forms the root of LuLing's superstitious beliefs because of how seriously her family takes the idea of curses and ghosts. They cannot take responsibility for their own complicity in harming others and forcing individuals to keep secrets, so they blame supernatural forces instead. There is also an implied misogyny in the way they treat both Precious Auntie and LuLing. Once LuLing's marriage is called off, she no longer has a role within the family or society at large. She is effectively banished, and when she gets to the orphanage, she realizes that the family has not even arranged for her to be taken in there. Part of LuLing's bitterness and suspicion comes from the abrupt abandonment she experiences at the hands of the Liu family. LuLing becomes self-reliant and unwilling to trust others.

Although she often felt ashamed of Precious Auntie, LuLing survives and even thrives because of how she was raised. At the most literal level, her ability to read and write gives her a marketable skill, which means that she can gradually build a respected career for herself as a teacher. She would never have had this ability if Precious Auntie had not passed ancestral knowledge down to her. LuLing can also adapt and make new friends because she has learned to be observant, intelligent, and resilient. LuLing previously blamed Precious Auntie for rendering her helpless and failing to teach her the skills LuLing thought she needed, but this turns out to be unfair.

PART TWO: EFFORTLESS, CHARACTER & FRAGRANCE

SUMMARY: EFFORTLESS

LuLing and Kai Jing meet in secret to kiss and touch each other. They make plans to marry, but these plans are interrupted by the news that Japanese soldiers have begun to invade China. On the morning the orphanage receives this news and tries to make sense of what will happen next, LuLing is astonished to see GaoLing arrive. GaoLing explains that she now lives in Peking with her husband, Fu Nan Chang. The family fortunes have gotten even worse, especially now that many of the sons have gone off to support military efforts. GaoLing snuck away from her husband and is in no hurry to return. Eventually, with the help of one of the nuns who runs the orphanage, GaoLing concocts a plan to lead her husband to believe that she has been arrested. She is then free to stay at the orphanage.

A few months later, LuLing and Kai Jing get married. The day is a mixture of happiness and fearfulness, since the threat of the Japanese invasion grows every day. LuLing and Kai Jing continue to work at the orphanage, with LuLing enjoying a close relationship with her father-in-law. However, after only a few months of happy marriage, Kai Jing and several of the other scientists are arrested by Chinese soldiers over their failure to enlist in the army. Eventually, the Japanese seize control of the area. This briefly allows Kai Jing and the others to return to the orphanage, but the next day, the Japanese come and arrest them again, convinced that they will be able to share the location of where the Chinese troops have fled. Kai Jing, along with others, is questioned and then executed.

SUMMARY: CHARACTER

LuLing mourns for Kai Jing, believing that her life no longer has any purpose. Eventually, the United States declares war on Japan, and Miss Grutoff is arrested as a prisoner of war. Before she leaves, she reveals that she has left money and instructions for how to evacuate the orphans to safe houses in Peking. Showing bravery and ingenuity, LuLing evacuates her group of orphans. Once they settle into new lives, GaoLing and LuLing move into some rooms in the back of the old ink shop, along with LuLing's father-in-law and one of the teachers from the school. The Chang family tolerates them living there because they implement several ideas that improve sales. Unfortunately, after the war ends, GaoLing's husband returns to claim her. He also announces that he has sold the ink shop. The others are resigned to finding somewhere else to live, but GaoLing refuses to give up her family business. Before a conclusion can be reached, they learn that Miss Grutoff has been released from the prisoner of war camp and is now very ill. They rush to see her and learn that she is planning to return to the US for medical treatment. There is an opportunity for one person to accompany her as her caregiver.

The group discusses who should go with Miss Grutoff, knowing that the chance to emigrate is a huge opportunity. LuLing is eager to go but puts on a pretense of being unwilling to leave GaoLing, but GaoLing agrees to go. The plan is that once she is in the US, she will sponsor LuLing to come be with her. In the meantime, LuLing will move to Hong Kong to wait. Teacher Pan will stay in Peking since he is considering remarrying. The group has a party to celebrate, imagining reuniting someday in the US.

SUMMARY: FRAGRANCE

> *I sailed for America, a land without curses or ghosts.*
> *By the time I landed, I was five years younger. Yet I felt*
> *so old.*
>
> *(See* QUOTATIONS, *p. 51)*

LuLing moves to Hong Kong, where she stays in a shabby rooming house. After a few months, she receives a letter from GaoLing with updates. Unfortunately, Miss Grutoff died almost as soon as they reached the US, and GaoLing learns that it will not be easy for her to sponsor LuLing. She works as a house cleaner and does not earn much money, and her family in China pressures her to send money home. GaoLing thinks her best chance is to find an American husband, and she is prepared to hide the fact that she is already married. LuLing is crushed and decides to return to Peking, but she learns that the train fare is now more than she can afford. She contemplates selling the bone, and when she takes it to several shops, she realizes that the bone is very valuable. She decides that she will not sell it and will instead work until she saves up enough money to pay for her train ticket.

LuLing moves into the cheapest accommodations she can find in Hong Kong and gets a job as a maid. She works in the home of two British women, Miss Patsy and Lady Ina. During the two years she works for them, LuLing learns English. GaoLing's letters mostly focus on how difficult her life in the US is, but one day she reports that she has met two brothers and thinks they might make good husbands for her and LuLing. As LuLing thinks about this possibility, she runs into Fu Nan Chang, who demands to know where his wife is. LuLing defiantly shares that GaoLing has gone to America but becomes alarmed when Fu Nan threatens to find her and tell people that she is already married. LuLing begins to pay off Fu Nan until she receives a letter from GaoLing saying that she has procured a visa for LuLing, and the Young brothers are interested in meeting her. Relieved, LuLing sells the bone and uses this money, along with her savings, to pay for her voyage to California.

ANALYSIS: EFFORTLESS, CHARACTER & FRAGRANCE

As LuLing grows older, economic and historical realities become more important influences in her life. In 1937, war broke out between Japan and China and would rage on until 1945, eventually becoming subsumed by the wider global conflict of World War II. Like the events around the discovery of the Peking Man, Tan only represents these events through the limited perspective of LuLing, who is not particularly politically savvy or interested in global affairs. However, these events affected the lives of everyone, even sheltered civilians. LuLing's life in the orphanage, which is American-run, provides her with some additional protection, but it cannot keep her young husband safe. Once the US declares war on Japan in December 1941, after the attack on Pearl Harbor, the Americans at the orphanage automatically become prisoners of war. Both during the war, and after it ends, LuLing also has to contend with economic consequences and how difficult the war makes it for her to earn a living and plan for her future.

LuLing's experience of romantic love is quickly followed by loss. She and Kai Jing build a relationship based on mutual love, desire, and respect. Even though she is young, LuLing feels a sense of agency and choice at a time when many marriages were arranged based on social and economic considerations. LuLing follows in her mother's footsteps by being empowered to marry the man of her choosing and feels genuine enthusiasm and desire for this relationship. LuLing learns that GaoLing married the man she had been intended for, and GaoLing has become trapped in an unhappy cycle of abuse. This news confirms that Precious Auntie was right all along and was able to effectively protect her daughter from marrying into the Chang family, even though it cost her life to do so. However, while LuLing enjoys a brief period of happiness, it is short-lived. Kai Jing's death foreshadows the death of her second husband as well. Knowing this tragic chapter of her history makes it more obvious why LuLing subsequently finds it difficult to open her heart and be emotionally intimate with others.

The surprising intersection of LuLing and GaoLing's adult lives suggests that GaoLing is a more complex character than originally shown. At first, GaoLing seemed like a docile and traditional foil for LuLing. However, she shows true loyalty and a mind of her own because she stands up for her "sister" even when no one else does. She shows herself to be resourceful and clever through her efforts to track down LuLing, even though it takes her years. GaoLing ends up in an unhappy marriage, but she does not passively accept her fate. She relies on her intelligence and a community of female allies to outwit her husband and live independently. In a parallel to LuLing, GaoLing finds ways to make her life better. This similarity between the two women helps to explain why they retain a lifelong bond. It also shows that under harsh and sometimes repressive conditions, women will still find ways to thrive.

The opportunity to immigrate to California represents a new horizon of hope for both GaoLing and LuLing. By this point, China has little to offer them. The loss of the Liu family's control over its business limits their economic opportunities, and at this time, they would be limited in the careers they could establish as unmarried women anyway. LuLing associates China with grief and the losses of her mother and her husband. GaoLing knows that if she stays, she will always be at risk of Fu Nan Chang finding and reclaiming her. Both women would have more uncertain futures but greater possibilities if they moved to a new country. Although they have endured a lot of suffering already, they retain some youthful optimism and innocence in terms of what they imagine America will be like.

The decision regarding which of them will go to America first reveals the mixture of loyalty and opportunism in GaoLing's character. She is sincere in her promise to bring LuLing to America, and she stays faithful to this commitment even though it requires years of waiting and hard work. However, GaoLing is more assertive and less committed to displays of politeness. She seizes the opportunity to be the first one to travel to California. Her boldness might reflect that she does not feel the same shame and self-loathing as LuLing does. Because LuLing is so traumatized by what happened with Precious Auntie, she tends to be more accepting of suffering and even feels that she deserves it. GaoLing, however, is always looking for ways to improve her situation and make her life as good as possible, whether it is by escaping her husband or moving to a new country.

While she waits to immigrate, LuLing enters a period of hard work and isolation but also a time when the true values of her character emerge. As a teenager, LuLing had been annoyed by Precious

Auntie's refusal to sell the oracle bone, but now she displays that same integrity and loyalty to her family's heritage. With so many connections to her past and her mother lost, the bone has taken on more value in her eyes. LuLing is no longer a spoiled and lazy girl, and she would choose years of hard work if it would allow her to live according to her values. However, LuLing is also not so rigid that she cannot compromise when necessary. She does eventually sell the bone to pay for her passage to join GaoLing. With the prospect of a new life ahead of her, LuLing decides to try and let her past go.

PART THREE: CHAPTERS ONE–THREE & EPILOGUE

SUMMARY: CHAPTER ONE

In the present day, Ruth has hired an elderly man named Mr. Tang to translate LuLing's narrative. Mr. Tang becomes fascinated with the story he uncovers. While he is working, Ruth stays at her mother's house. Art is initially worried by this decision, fearing that it reflects her being unhappy with their relationship. To explain to LuLing why she is moving in with her, Ruth says that she is working on a children's book and wants LuLing to do the illustrations. Living with her mother gives Ruth the sense that she is reverting to an earlier version of herself. It also gives her the chance to reflect on her relationship with Art, and she is pleased to see that both he and the girls seem to miss her more than she expected.

Mr. Tang calls to tell Ruth that he has finished the translation, although he is curious about whether there is more to the document. Ruth invites him to come to dinner so that he can deliver the translation and meet LuLing in person. Because of what he knows about her past, Mr. Tang reminisces with LuLing as if they are old friends. As soon as he leaves, Ruth reads the document, realizing that some of what she interpreted as signs that LuLing was confused was actually rooted in real history. She now has a new perspective on her mother and their relationship.

The next day, Ruth phones Art and tells him what she has learned. Art shares that he has been reflecting on their relationship and the future. He asks Ruth if she would consider finding an assisted living facility for LuLing. Ruth is initially resistant, but she is touched that Art is taking an interest in the situation. Art fakes a letter claiming that there are signs of dangerous chemical levels near LuLing's house and that the local government is going to pay for her to stay at a "luxury residence" for several months. This way, Ruth and Art can secretly get LuLing to give the assisted living home a chance. Ruth is impressed with the commitment Art shows to the plan. She and Art go and visit the residence he selects, and Ruth is impressed with the facilities but horrified by the cost. Art reassures her that he is happy to cover the cost and urges Ruth to be more accepting when people show her kindness and love. LuLing seems happy to move to the facility, especially once Art and Ruth convince her that she is getting a better deal than everyone else.

SUMMARY: CHAPTER TWO

The family gathers to celebrate GaoLing's birthday. Ruth manages to find a moment alone with GaoLing and mentions a few of the details she has learned from reading her mother's manuscript. GaoLing assumes that LuLing has finally shared this information with her daughter. GaoLing explains that she always thought it was fine to simply tell the truth, but LuLing insisted on keeping the secret. Edmund is the only one who knows the truth. Ruth tells GaoLing about the manuscript, which she believes LuLing wrote seven or eight years ago, possibly when she began to be concerned about her own memory. She also mentions the idea of LuLing moving into a care home. GaoLing initially objects, but Ruth persuades her to visit the facility. Ruth says that she will not make any decisions without GaoLing's approval. She also wants GaoLing to read the document.

GaoLing provides additional details about individuals mentioned in the manuscript. Chang was arrested after the war for shady business practices and executed. Most of his family was left penniless, and Fu Nan eventually died. GaoLing has never told anyone about her first husband. GaoLing explains that when her father-in-law died, she and Edmund felt bad about LuLing only being left a small amount of money. They split the inheritance and gave her half, but LuLing never spent the money. She invested it so that it has grown over time. However, GaoLing cannot remember the key piece of information Ruth wants: Precious Auntie's real name. The conversation ends abruptly when LuLing falls into the swimming pool and has to be rescued by Art. The next day, Ruth moves some of her mother's items to the assisted living home. That night, she and Art have dinner. They discuss their love for one another and their desire to move to a new stage of their relationship where they will be more honest and emotionally intimate.

SUMMARY: CHAPTER THREE

> *Her grandmother had a name. Gu Liu Xin. She had existed. She still existed. Precious Auntie belonged to a family. LuLing belonged to that same family, and Ruth belonged to them both.*
>
> *(See QUOTATIONS, p. 51)*

The narrative resumes about a month later. LuLing lives happily at the assisted living home and enjoys a new relationship with Mr. Tang. One day, Mr. Tang takes LuLing, Ruth, and Art to a museum where he shows them an ancient bone object. LuLing recognizes it as the "oracle bone" she once owned and sold. As LuLing drifts into the recollection, she shares her mother's name: Gu Liu Xin. At first, Ruth is elated, but then she realizes that since "gu" is the Chinese word for "bone," her mother must simply be confused. She feels defeated, wondering if she will ever know the family name of her maternal grandmother. However, Ruth is heartened by the relationship developing between her mother and Mr. Tang. That night, Art suggests that he and Ruth consider marriage.

A few days later, GaoLing phones Ruth. She reached out to family members in China and asked them to do some research. They confirmed that LuLing's mother was named Liu Xin Gu. Her father was Dr. Gu, but the sound for "gu" can mean several things, including "bone." Ruth realizes that she can finally have a clear connection to her grandmother.

SUMMARY: EPILOGUE

On August 12, one year after the story began, Ruth again observes her annual silence. She has not lost her voice, but she chooses to focus on writing rather than speaking. LuLing recently reached out to apologize for some of her past behavior, and Ruth reassured her that she loved and forgave her. With the new understanding of her family history, Ruth feels more compassion for her mother and herself. She is now writing a book of her own.

ANALYSIS: CHAPTERS ONE–THREE & EPILOGUE

Surprisingly, Ruth's decision to become closer to her mother affects her relationship with Art before it affects her relationship with LuLing. Art has grown accustomed to having all of his needs met in the relationship, and he is used to having Ruth put herself second. Therefore, it surprises him when Ruth moves out to be with LuLing. Without Ruth around to oversee daily domestic responsibilities, Art and his daughters quickly realize just how valuable Ruth has been and how little they have appreciated her. Art's new appreciation for Ruth causes him to reflect on the emotional dynamic in their relationship. He is able to communicate that he feels like Ruth has never been fully open with him, and Ruth, having just read her mother's manuscript, can recognize the truth in this. When she reads the manuscript, Ruth realizes how much her mother has hidden and what this has meant for Ruth. Ruth has unwittingly imitated LuLing's behavior of hiding true feelings and desires. In fact, as Ruth admits to Art, she doesn't even know what she truly wants.

Once she understands who LuLing truly is, Ruth can begin the work of trying to understand her identity and what she wants her future to look like. Her relationship with Art has always been partially stalled, but now it can move forward. Through this relationship, Tan implies that when people are missing a connection to their past, they cannot fully embrace their future. After a trial separation, Ruth and Art both become more grateful for one another and more committed to moving forward in their relationship. This deepened partnership allows them to work together on their plan to move LuLing into an assisted living facility. Significantly, Art is the one who comes up with this idea.

Art is also the one who orchestrates the plan to deceive LuLing. On one hand, the deception is relatively harmless and actually improves LuLing's quality of life. On the other, the plan relies on a lie at a moment when the plot of the novel shows just how important honesty is. Ruth finally knows LuLing for the first time, with no secrets and no lies, and yet she immediately introduces a falsehood into their relationship. Indeed, Ruth begins to enjoy the plot to trick LuLing because it helps her feel closer to Art. Once her relationship with Art improves, he arguably becomes the most important person in her life. This might represent a healthy maturation in which Ruth can finally separate her identity from her relationship with her mother, but it also marks a moment where she chooses loyalty to Art over a truly honest relationship with LuLing. At the same time, the deception is only possible because of how well Ruth knows LuLing, and, in this sense, it reflects the intimacy of truly knowing someone's character and what is important to them.

Mr. Tang represents the possibility of a new start for LuLing and shows the effect that honesty and transparency can have. Even before he meets her, Mr. Tang is infatuated with LuLing, which shows that admiration can develop based on knowledge of someone's past rather than their present. A close bond grows between the elderly couple because Mr. Tang is the first person in years who truly knows everything there is to know about LuLing. In a sense, that makes her feel as if he has been part of her life for years. It is also telling that when Mr. Tang knows the truth about LuLing's past, he falls in love with her. LuLing has hidden her secrets for years because she believed people would shame and reject her if they knew the truth. She inherited this legacy of shame and secrecy because of how Precious Auntie was forced to hide the truth about her life. However, with both Ruth and Mr. Tang, the truth is what makes people see LuLing clearly and respect and admire her for everything she has lived through.

The new information about her mother results in an inward change more than an outer one for Ruth. Because of LuLing's declining cognitive state, Ruth does not discuss what she has learned with her or ask additional questions. This lack of conversation shows the loss associated with delay. Ruth is more fortunate than LuLing was in that she learns the truth about her mother while her mother is still alive, but it is still too late for her and LuLing to truly achieve a new type of relationship. LuLing is now suffering from dementia and cannot discuss the manuscript with Ruth. Still, LuLing does seem to experience a new kind of peacefulness. For the first time, the people around her have the context to understand what she is trying to communicate, and she can make references to her past. LuLing is no longer alone with her story, and Ruth has new knowledge that enriches her own life.

Because she cannot discuss the manuscript with her mother, Ruth makes choices for herself about how she wants to honor her mother and grandmother. These choices are especially significant because Ruth does not have her own daughter. Ruth's decision to not have children is not discussed in detail, but she does reflect that she feared repeating the same patterns LuLing established when raising her. Ruth has thus broken the chain of mothers transmitting their pain but also their strength to their daughters. Perhaps because of this, she becomes determined to learn the true name of her maternal grandmother. So much about Precious Auntie has already been lost. There will never be a grave or a commemoration for her, and as

LuLing's memory fades, the last traces of her will be lost. By learning her name, Ruth wants to assert her grandmother's existence and preserve her legacy.

When she finally learns her grandmother's name, Ruth feels a sense of peace because she can now understand her own identity and history in ways she has previously pushed aside. Ruth's extended family has always been tied to her father's family, but now she has balance. This reclamation of her female lineage empowers Ruth to find her voice and be more assertive. This affects her professionally as well as personally. Not only does her relationship with Art become much more open and equitable, but Ruth also begins to write her own book, rather than simply revise the stories of others. The new relationship to her mother and grandmother's history gives her the confidence to finally articulate herself. Ruth becomes a mirror of her grandmother in that she continues to observe a period of silence so that she can focus on communicating through writing. Spoken words are temporary and vanish quickly, but as the novel has shown, written words can endure and provide truth for generations to come.

Important Quotations Explained

1. In an odd way, she now thought, her mother was the one who had taught her to become a book doctor. Ruth had to make life better by revising it.

This quotation occurs when the adult Ruth is reflecting on some of the unhappy and embarrassing memories from her childhood. Because LuLing's English was limited, as a child, Ruth often had to act as a translator for her mother, and she took these opportunities to soften or disguise the message LuLing wanted to convey. By "revising" what LuLing was trying to say, Ruth could control how her mother—and thus she herself—was perceived. Ruth found this translating role both frustrating and comforting because she could exert some control over her mother, whom she found embarrassing and irrational. She wanted to make her mother "better" in her American world. However, the truth cannot be revised and still remain truthful, and Ruth has always suffered from her attempts to speak for others.

Now, as a ghostwriter, Ruth takes the ideas of someone else and decides how best to communicate them. She sees this ability as a skill she learned from living with LuLing. Again, she takes someone's thoughts and revises them to be more palatable and useful to others. However, what Ruth does not yet acknowledge is that this focus on conveying others' messages leaves her without the ability to speak her own ideas and desires. Ruth secretly dreams of writing her own book but lacks the courage to do so, and her focus on her mother often distracts her from thinking about her own happiness and identity. Ruth sees herself as just revising the stories of others rather than having the agency to write her own. This quotation also alludes to the family secret that will eventually set Ruth free to claim her agency and identity. When she whimsically refers to herself as a "book doctor," she does not yet know that she comes from a lineage of healers through her grandmother, the bonesetter's daughter.

2.   She recalled that when her younger self stood on this
        same beach for the first time, she had thought the sand
        looked like a gigantic writing surface. The slate was clean,
        inviting, open to possibilities. And at that moment of her
        life, she had a new determination, a fierce hope.

This quotation occurs when Ruth goes to the beach at Land's End
and recalls the first time she visited this location when she was
eleven years old and had just moved to San Francisco with her
mother. Their move was associated with escaping from Ruth's past
trauma of being pursued by Lance, and it helped her to achieve a
sense of healing through establishing a new life for herself. Ruth
had persuaded her mother to move to San Francisco by pretending that Precious Auntie was sending LuLing a message, when in
reality, Ruth was controlling the narrative and creating a way out
of a frightening situation for herself. Ruth's first visit to the beach
marked the moment when she realized she had agency and created
a new future for herself. Up until this point, Ruth had been passive
and vulnerable. She mainly existed as a reflection of her mother and
her friends. But, through this move, Ruth sets the stage for her later
life as a rebellious teenager who challenges the value system she has
grown up with.

The quotation also foreshadows Ruth's future career and links
her to her past, which she does not yet understand. The comparison of the beach to a writing surface hints at her future job as a
ghostwriter. Though Ruth finds the sand slate inviting, sand is
also changeable and can be washed away easily. Ruth's career in
the shadows of the literary world will mirror this mutability. The
writing surface of the sand also reflects how both her mother and
grandmother were skilled painters and calligraphers, but their gifts
have been washed away by the tides of violence in their lives. Ruth
looks at the beach and imagines writing her own story, but she does
not yet know that LuLing and Precious Auntie have left narratives
of their own for her, through which she will discover a much more
permanent family history.

3.   In this way, Precious Auntie taught me to be naughty, just
like her. She taught me to be curious, just like her. She
taught me to be spoiled. And because I was all these things,
she could not teach me to be a better daughter, though, in
the end, she tried to change my faults.

This quotation comes from LuLing's narrative of the past, when she
describes a moment in her childhood when Precious Auntie play-
fully mocked the other more reserved women in their family. The
quotation shows LuLing's understanding of how her close relationship with Precious Auntie shaped her identity and character. Even
though, at this point, LuLing did not know that Precious Auntie
was her biological mother, Precious Auntie influenced her more
than the other adults because of how much time the two of them
spent together. Precious Auntie had an unusual childhood because
her father gave her a lot of independence and ensured that she was
well-educated. This childhood made Precious Auntie confident and
resilient, which proved very valuable after she encountered tremendous pain and suffering in her life. Precious Auntie passed this same
perspective on to her daughter, even though she was not allowed to
tell LuLing the true nature of their relationship.

LuLing describes the qualities she learns from Precious Auntie
as being mainly negative, but she fails to see how they eventually
benefited her. LuLing is haunted by regret and grief because she
thinks her stubborn and arrogant ways led to her mother's suicide.
While her headstrong behavior may have contributed to the tragic
event, it also gave her the self-reliance to survive being sent to the
orphanage, living through a war, moving to a foreign country,
losing two husbands, and raising a child as a single mother. If
LuLing had been more passive or more traditional, she might not
have been able to rise to these challenges. LuLing is so trapped by
shame and regret that she cannot recognize her own strengths and
value. Because LuLing has shame and negative associations with the
qualities she displayed as a young girl, she also lashes out when she
sees her own daughter displaying the same qualities. Ruth cannot
understand why her mother is so harsh with her, but this description
of the shame LuLing feels around her past behavior sheds light on
why LuLing is so afraid of her daughter becoming independent and
free-thinking.

4.   I sailed for America, a land without curses or ghosts. By
     the time I landed, I was five years younger. Yet I felt so old.

This quotation comes from the end of LuLing's narrative when she
leaves China behind to move to the US. It reveals both her hopes for
her future and her tremendous sense of loss. Like many immigrants,
LuLing pictures America as a new world and imagines it as a land
of opportunity. She has, in fact, worked hard for years in order to
join GaoLing there. Much of LuLing's life and worldview have been
shaped by a relationship to the past where previous generations still
exert significant influence. Bad actions could have consequences for
generations, and LuLing understands that many of the things that
have impacted her life have been linked to events set in motion years
earlier. Thus, LuLing hopes that by moving to a new place where no
one will know her identity or history, she will be able to break free
from the family cycle of tragedy and loss. However, the comment is
ironic because LuLing will always carry her psychological trauma
with her. She will never be able to forget or forgive herself for what
happened to Precious Auntie. In fact, LuLing will end up longing for
contact with her mother's spirit and believing that she can receive
messages transmitted through Ruth. When LuLing comments that
she felt old, she hints at the way she has been indelibly shaped by
the tragic events she has lived through. LuLing might hope that the
move to America will bring a completely fresh start, but it is clear
that the first part of her life will always affect her. Though she sails
for California in an attempt to turn back time, her emotional pain
will always make her feel "old" before her time.

5.   Her grandmother had a name. Gu Liu Xin. She had
      existed. She still existed. Precious Auntie belonged to a
      family. LuLing belonged to that same family, and Ruth
      belonged to them both.

This quotation comes from the very end of the novel when Ruth finally learns the true name of her maternal grandmother. The quotation reveals that Ruth feels complete now that she has learned the history of her mother and grandmother. By uncovering her grandmother's name, Ruth feels a true connection with her, a proof of her existence beyond the tales in her mother's manuscript. Ruth also ensures that her grandmother's memory will live on and that Precious Auntie will be remembered in a more complex way. She was not simply a scarred nursemaid but a woman with her own history, secrets, strength, and desires.

Precious Auntie's name is also significant in that it reflects her family's profession as bonesetters. "Gu" is both the family's surname and the Chinese word for "bone," which demonstrates how intrinsic the family profession and history are to each family member's identity. Bones can break, but they can also heal. Precious Auntie and LuLing demonstrated this by surviving loss and grief, and Ruth sees now that she also possesses the strength of her female ancestors. Ruth also learns that she comes from a lineage of bonesetters whose skills have now vanished from the family history, and Ruth wants to commemorate and honor those traditions. Because she knows the true stories of her mother and grandmother, Ruth can see how they have influenced and shaped her. When Ruth thinks that Precious Auntie "still existed," she does not mean this literally. Rather, she means that she can see aspects of her grandmother in herself, and that she will ensure that her grandmother's story and memory are passed along for future generations.

KEY FACTS

FULL TITLE
The Bonesetter's Daughter

AUTHOR
Amy Tan

TYPE OF WORK
Novel

GENRE
Literary fiction; family drama; historical fiction

LANGUAGE
English

TIME AND PLACE WRITTEN
Mid–late 1990s, San Francisco and New York City

DATE OF FIRST PUBLICATION
2001

PUBLISHER
Random House

NARRATOR
The present-day sections of the novel are narrated by an anonymous narrator, while the sections describing LuLing's life are narrated by LuLing.

POINT OF VIEW
The novel consists of a narrative, written by LuLing, nested within the larger plot of Ruth's present life. The anonymous narrator speaks in the third person, relating only what Ruth can see and hear and providing a subjective perspective of what Ruth thinks and feels. In the narrative section, LuLing speaks in the first person, describing her own thoughts, feelings, and motivations.

TONE

The tone of the anonymous narrator is compassionate and nonjudgmental in describing Ruth, LuLing, and the conflict between them. The tone of LuLing's narrative is wistful, pained, and regretful as she describes tragic events from her past.

TENSE

The main plot of the novel is written in the present tense, but the narrative describing LuLing's life is written in the past tense.

SETTING (TIME)

Ruth's portion of the novel takes place in the late twentieth-century. LuLing's history includes events that take place between approximately 1900 and the late 1940s.

SETTING (PLACE)

San Francisco and China

PROTAGONIST

Ruth Young

MAJOR CONFLICT

Ruth struggles to understand and feel compassion for her mother because LuLing has often been harsh with her and because Ruth does not know much about LuLing's past.

RISING ACTION

Ruth's struggle to relate to her mother begins in her childhood when they often fight and continues as adult Ruth becomes increasingly worried about her elderly mother and has to take on the role of caregiver.

CLIMAX

The climax occurs when Ruth reads the manuscript narrating her mother's life. At this point, Ruth's struggle to understand LuLing becomes overt because she realizes how little she has known about her mother and how much this ignorance has shaped her inability to relate to LuLing.

FALLING ACTION

After Ruth reads the manuscript, she becomes much more respectful of and patient with LuLing, and she becomes committed to discovering Precious Auntie's true name so that she can honor her memory and ensure that it will live on.

KEY FACTS

THEMES
   Mother–daughter relationships; resilience; secrecy

MOTIFS
   Bones; ghosts; suicide

SYMBOLS
   The pearl necklace; Precious Auntie's scars; the oracle bone

FORESHADOWING
   Precious Auntie's childhood with no siblings and one parent
   foreshadows Ruth's childhood family; Baby Uncle's accident
   when he breaks his toe foreshadows his death in another
   incident with a horse; Baby Uncle's death foreshadows the
   death of Edmund Young; Precious Auntie's suicide foreshadows
   LuLing's suicide attempt and Ruth's suicidal thoughts.

KEY FACTS

STUDY QUESTIONS

1. *How does Ruth's view of romantic love compare with the perspectives of her mother and grandmother?*

Though in many ways they were unusually independent Chinese women for their time, Precious Auntie and LuLing had their romantic decisions influenced by economic and social concerns. Precious Auntie's father allowed her a great sense of autonomy, and Precious Auntie made the independent choice to marry Baby Uncle because she was attracted to him. However, she paid for this choice with a lot of pain and suffering because she offended her other suitor Chang's pride. Chang, representing the traditional misogyny of society, punished Precious Auntie by organizing an attack on her father and Baby Uncle. Like her mother, LuLing had some agency in selecting a husband, but, unlike Precious Auntie, LuLing was interested in marriage for economic stability and social opportunity. Therefore, she considered the union with Fu Nan Chang that eventually drove Precious Auntie to suicide. Love did drive LuLing to marry her first husband, Kai Jing, but their loving marriage was destroyed by war, reflecting the unlikelihood of female agency and happiness in traditional Chinese society.

In contrast with her mother and grandmother, Ruth is free to choose a partner on the basis of compatibility and happiness without as much societal judgment. When Ruth first meets Art, she does not think of him as a prospective romantic partner at all. In fact, she believes he is gay and that he is only interested in her as a friend. Ruth gets to know him as a person, and the question of romantic attraction only comes later. Ruth chooses to pursue a relationship with Art because she enjoys spending time with him, but she is already economically independent and does not want to have children. She is happy in her relationship even though Art is not Chinese, and he approaches the world with Western values. Though Ruth and Art are at first emotionally distant, by the end of the novel, they establish a mutual partnership and, through this, Ruth's relationship represents a significant step toward marital happiness for the women of her family.

2.   *How does the relationship between LuLing and*
     GaoLing change over time?

LuLing and GaoLing's relationship begins as relatively distant, becomes closer due to LuLing's suffering, and then becomes ambivalent due to GaoLing's ambition. Even though they are extremely close in age, GaoLing and LuLing are not very close as young children. LuLing spends most of her time with Precious Auntie, and she sometimes resents GaoLing for being their mother's favorite. However, their relationship changes when Precious Auntie kills herself and LuLing becomes ostracized by the family. GaoLing is the only one to show kindness to her, and even after LuLing is banished to the orphanage, GaoLing never gives up. She spends years searching for her sister. On the one hand, this loyalty shows that GaoLing loves LuLing and is not ashamed of her. On the other, during this time, GaoLing is trapped in an unhappy marriage, and her relationship with LuLing gives her an opportunity to gain more independence and freedom.

GaoLing's ambitious and somewhat opportunistic perspective makes the relationship between the sisters become more ambivalent over time. GaoLing tricks LuLing into giving up the opportunity to be the first to immigrate to America. Then, after GaoLing ends up with greater economic stability and social position due to her husband prospering and LuLing's husband dies, she sometimes makes insensitive comments to LuLing. Both women grew up in an era in which making an advantageous marriage and achieving a comfortable life were highly desirable, so they continue to be competitive with one another in this realm. However, even though they squabble, GaoLing remains loyal to her sister. She keeps all of LuLing's secrets, is always willing to help her, and ensures that LuLing gets an equal share of the Young family inheritance. Just like relationships between mothers and daughters, relationships between sisters are complicated but also profound and enduring.

STUDY QUESTIONS

3.   *Why does Ruth feel disconnected from her mother and
      her family heritage?*

Ruth feels disconnected from her mother and family heritage
because she lacks knowledge of LuLing's history. Until she reads the
manuscript LuLing has written, Ruth is ignorant about what her
mother has lived through and the suffering she has experienced. She
does not know that LuLing lives with grief and guilt every day and
that this explains some of her erratic behavior. For example, Ruth
has always been embarrassed by her mother's obsession with con-
tacting the spirit of Precious Auntie. She has always believed that
LuLing was ignorant and outdated for trying to contact a ghost.
Because Ruth thinks of herself as a modern, rational woman, she
feels like she is very different from her mother. However, when
Ruth gains more knowledge about LuLing's life, she sees that many
of LuLing's actions actually make sense in context. She also gains
appreciation for how hard LuLing has worked to give her a good
life, and she feels a deeper mother-daughter connection because she
recognizes that everything she has comes from the sacrifices and suffering of her mother and grandmother.

Ruth also gains a deeper sense of familial connection when
she is able to see the similarities between herself and her mother
and grandmother. Ruth and LuLing are both the only children of
a woman who had to be very independent while hiding away her
grief and pain. Precious Auntie could never tell her daughter her
true identity, and LuLing kept her life in China secret from Ruth.
All three women are intelligent, educated, and interested in writing
and art. Both LuLing and Precious Auntie followed their hearts and
had relationships with men they loved at a time when this was not
always allowed for women. Knowing these things about LuLing
and Precious Auntie, Ruth gains more respect for them and is also
able to see how they are not so different from herself. She can actually understand who she is by learning the history of the women
who came before her. In fact, by the end of the novel, Ruth understands that it is only by embracing her family lineage that she can
actually arrive at deeper self-awareness.

STUDY QUESTIONS

How to Write Literary Analysis

The Literary Essay: A Step-by-Step Guide

When you read for pleasure, your only goal is enjoyment. You might find yourself reading to get caught up in an exciting story, to learn about an interesting time or place, or just to pass time. Maybe you're looking for inspiration, guidance, or a reflection of your own life. There are as many different, valid ways of reading a book as there are books in the world.

When you read a work of literature in an English class, however, you're being asked to read in a special way: you're being asked to perform *literary analysis*. To analyze something means to break it down into smaller parts and then examine how those parts work, both individually and together. Literary analysis involves examining all the parts of a novel, play, short story, or poem—elements such as character, setting, tone, and imagery—and thinking about how the author uses those elements to create certain effects.

A literary essay isn't a book review: you're not being asked whether or not you liked a book or whether you'd recommend it to another reader. A literary essay also isn't like the kind of book report you wrote when you were younger, when your teacher wanted you to summarize the book's action. A high school or college–level literary essay asks, "How does this piece of literature actually work?" "How does it do what it does?" and, "Why might the author have made the choices he or she did?"

The Seven Steps

No one is born knowing how to analyze literature; it's a skill and a process you can master. As you gain more practice with this kind of thinking and writing, you'll be able to craft a method that works best for you. But until then, here are seven basic steps to writing a well-constructed literary essay:

>   *1. Ask questions*
>   *2. Collect evidence*
>   *3. Construct a thesis*

4. Develop and organize arguments
5. Write the introduction
6. Write the body paragraphs
7. Write the conclusion

1. Ask Questions

When you're assigned a literary essay in class, your teacher will often provide you with a list of writing prompts. Lucky you! Now all you have to do is choose one. Do yourself a favor and pick a topic that interests you. You'll have a much better (not to mention easier) time if you start off with something you enjoy thinking about. If you are asked to come up with a topic by yourself, though, you might start to feel a little panicked. Maybe you have too many ideas—or none at all. Don't worry. Take a deep breath and start by asking yourself these questions:

- **What struck you?** Did a particular image, line, or scene linger in your mind for a long time? If it fascinated you, chances are you can draw on it to write a fascinating essay.

- **What confused you?** Maybe you were surprised to see a character act in a certain way, or maybe you didn't understand why the book ended the way it did. Confusing moments in a work of literature are like a loose thread in a sweater: if you pull on it, you can unravel the entire thing. Ask yourself why the author chose to write about that character or scene the way he or she did, and you might tap into some important insights about the work as a whole.

- **Did you notice any patterns?** Is there a phrase that the main character uses constantly or an image that repeats throughout the book? If you can figure out how that pattern weaves through the work and what the significance of that pattern is, you've almost got your entire essay mapped out.

- **Did you notice any contradictions or ironies?** Great works of literature are complex; great literary essays recognize and explain those complexities. Maybe the title of the work seems to contradict its content (for example, the play *Happy Days* shows its two characters buried up to their waists in dirt). Maybe the main character acts one way around his or her family and a completely different way around his or her friends and associates. If you can find a way to explain

a work's contradictory elements, you've got the seeds of a
great essay.

At this point, you don't need to know exactly what you're going to
say about your topic; you just need a place to begin your exploration.
You can help direct your reading and brainstorming by formulating
your topic as a *question*, which you'll then try to answer in your
essay. The best questions invite critical debates and discussions,
not just a rehashing of the summary. Remember, you're looking for
something you can *prove or argue* based on evidence you find in the
text. Finally, remember to keep the scope of your question in mind:
is this a topic you can adequately address within the word or page
limit you've been given? Conversely, is this a topic big enough to fill
the required length?

GOOD QUESTIONS

> *"Are Romeo and Juliet's parents responsible for the
> deaths of their children?"*
> *"Why do pigs keep showing up in* Lord of the Flies?"
> *"Are Dr. Frankenstein and his monster alike? How?"*

BAD QUESTIONS

> *"What happens to Scout in* To Kill a Mockingbird?"
> *"What do the other characters in* Julius Caesar *think
> about Caesar?"*
> *"How does Hester Prynne in* The Scarlet Letter *remind
> me of my sister?"*

---

2. COLLECT EVIDENCE

Once you know what question you want to answer, it's time to scour
the book for things that will help you answer the question. Don't
worry if you don't know what you want to say yet—right now
you're just collecting ideas and material and letting it all percolate.
Keep track of passages, symbols, images, or scenes that deal with
your topic. Eventually, you'll start making connections between
these examples, and your thesis will emerge.

Here's a brief summary of the various parts that compose each
and every work of literature. These are the elements that you will
analyze in your essay and that you will offer as evidence to support
your arguments. For more on the parts of literary works, see the
Glossary of Literary Terms at the end of this section.

ELEMENTS OF STORY   These are the *what*s of the work—what happens, where it happens, and to whom it happens.

- **Plot:** All the events and actions of the work.

- **Character:** The people who act and are acted on in a literary work. The main character of a work is known as the *protagonist*.

- **Conflict:** The central tension in the work. In most cases, the protagonist wants something, while opposing forces (antagonists) hinder the protagonist's progress.

- **Setting:** When and where the work takes place. Elements of setting include location, time period, time of day, weather, social atmosphere, and economic conditions.

- **Narrator:** The person telling the story. The narrator may straightforwardly report what happens, convey the subjective opinions and perceptions of one or more characters, or provide commentary and opinion in his or her own voice.

- **Themes:** The main idea or message of the work—usually an abstract idea about people, society, or life in general. A work may have many themes, which may be in tension with one another.

ELEMENTS OF STYLE   These are the *how*s—how the characters speak, how the story is constructed, and how language is used throughout the work.

- **Structure and organization:** How the parts of the work are assembled. Some novels are narrated in a linear, chronological fashion, while others skip around in time. Some plays follow a traditional three- or five-act structure, while others are a series of loosely connected scenes. Some authors deliberately leave gaps in their work, leaving readers to puzzle out the missing information. A work's structure and organization can tell you a lot about the kind of message it wants to convey.

- **Point of view:** The perspective from which a story is told. In *first-person point of view*, the narrator involves himself or herself in the story. ("I went to the store"; "We watched in horror as the bird slammed into the window.") A first-person narrator is usually the protagonist of the work, but not always. In *third-person point of view*, the narrator does not participate

LITERARY ANALYSIS

in the story. A third-person narrator may closely follow a specific character, recounting that individual character's thoughts or experiences, or it may be what we call an *omniscient* narrator. Omniscient narrators see and know all: they can witness any event in any time or place and are privy to the inner thoughts and feelings of all characters. Remember that the narrator and the author are not the same thing!

- **Diction:** Word choice. Whether a character uses dry, clinical language or flowery prose with lots of exclamation points can tell you a lot about his or her attitude and personality.

- **Syntax:** Word order and sentence construction. Syntax is a crucial part of establishing an author's narrative voice. Ernest Hemingway, for example, is known for writing in very short, straightforward sentences, while James Joyce characteristically wrote in long, extremely complicated lines.

- **Tone:** The mood or feeling of the text. Diction and syntax often contribute to the tone of a work. A novel written in short, clipped sentences that use small, simple words might feel brusque, cold, or matter-of-fact.

- **Imagery:** Language that appeals to the senses, representing things that can be seen, smelled, heard, tasted, or touched.

- **Figurative language:** Language that is not meant to be interpreted literally. The most common types of figurative language are *metaphors* and *similes*, which compare two unlike things in order to suggest a similarity between them— for example, "All the world's a stage," or "The moon is like a ball of green cheese." (Metaphors say one thing *is* another thing; similes claim that one thing is *like* another thing.)

---

3. CONSTRUCT A THESIS

When you've examined all the evidence you've collected and know how you want to answer the question, it's time to write your thesis statement. A *thesis* is a claim about a work of literature that needs to be supported by evidence and arguments. The thesis statement is the heart of the literary essay, and the bulk of your paper will be spent trying to prove this claim. A good thesis will be:

- **Arguable.** "*The Great Gatsby* describes New York society in the 1920s" isn't a thesis—it's a fact.

- **Provable through textual evidence.** "*Hamlet* is a confusing but ultimately very well-written play" is a weak thesis because it offers the writer's personal opinion about the book. Yes, it's arguable, but it's not a claim that can be proved or supported with examples taken from the play itself.

- **Surprising.** "Both George and Lenny change a great deal in *Of Mice and Men*" is a weak thesis because it's obvious. A really strong thesis will argue for a reading of the text that is not immediately apparent.

- **Specific.** "Dr. Frankenstein's monster tells us a lot about the human condition" is *almost* a really great thesis statement, but it's still too vague. What does the writer mean by "a lot"? *How* does the monster tell us so much about the human condition?

GOOD THESIS STATEMENTS

Question: In *Romeo and Juliet*, which is more powerful in shaping the lovers' story: fate or foolishness?

Thesis: "Though Shakespeare defines Romeo and Juliet as 'star-crossed lovers,' and images of stars and planets appear throughout the play, a closer examination of that celestial imagery reveals that the stars are merely witnesses to the characters' foolish activities and not the causes themselves."

Question: How does the bell jar function as a symbol in Sylvia Plath's *The Bell Jar*?

Thesis: "A bell jar is a bell-shaped glass that has three basic uses: to hold a specimen for observation, to contain gases, and to maintain a vacuum. The bell jar appears in each of these capacities in *The Bell Jar*, Plath's semi-autobiographical novel, and each appearance marks a different stage in Esther's mental breakdown."

Question: Would Piggy in *The Lord of the Flies* make a good island leader if he were given the chance?

Thesis: "Though the intelligent, rational, and innovative Piggy has the mental characteristics of a good leader, he ultimately lacks the social skills necessary to be an effective one. Golding emphasizes this point by giving Piggy a foil in the charismatic Jack, whose magnetic personality allows him to capture and wield power effectively, if not always wisely."

LITERARY ANALYSIS

4. DEVELOP AND ORGANIZE ARGUMENTS

The reasons and examples that support your thesis will form the middle paragraphs of your essay. Since you can't really write your thesis statement until you know how you'll structure your argument, you'll probably end up working on steps 3 and 4 at the same time. There's no single method of argumentation that will work in every context. One essay prompt might ask you to compare and contrast two characters, while another asks you to trace an image through a given work of literature. These questions require different kinds of answers and therefore different kinds of arguments. Below, we'll discuss three common kinds of essay prompts and some strategies for constructing a solid, well-argued case.

TYPES OF LITERARY ESSAYS

- **Compare and contrast**

  Compare and contrast the characters of Huck and Jim in The Adventures of Huckleberry Finn.

  Chances are you've written this kind of essay before. In an academic literary context, you'll organize your arguments the same way you would in any other class. You can either go *subject by subject* or *point by point*. In the former, you'll discuss one character first and then the second. In the latter, you'll choose several traits (attitude toward life, social status, images and metaphors associated with the character) and devote a paragraph to each. You may want to use a mix of these two approaches—for example, you may want to spend a paragraph apiece broadly sketching Huck's and Jim's personalities before transitioning to a paragraph or two describing a few key points of comparison. This can be a highly effective strategy if you want to make a counterintuitive argument—that, despite seeming to be totally different, the two characters or objects being compared are actually similar in a very important way (or vice versa). Remember that your essay should reveal something fresh or unexpected about the text, so think beyond the obvious parallels and differences.

- **Trace**

  Choose an image—for example, birds, knives, or eyes—and trace that image throughout Macbeth.

  Sounds pretty easy, right? All you need to do is read the play, underline every appearance of a knife in *Macbeth* and then list them in your essay in the order they appear, right? Well, not exactly. Your teacher doesn't want a simple catalog of examples. He or she wants to see you make *connections* between those examples—that's the difference between summarizing and analyzing. In the *Macbeth* example, think about the different contexts in which knives appear in the play and to what effect. In *Macbeth*, there are real knives and imagined knives; knives that kill and knives that simply threaten. Categorize and classify your examples to give them some order. Finally, always keep the overall effect in mind. After you choose and analyze your examples, you should come to some greater understanding about the work, as well as the role of your chosen image, symbol, or phrase in developing the major themes and stylistic strategies of that work.

- **Debate**

  Is the society depicted in 1984 *good for its citizens?*

  In this kind of essay, you're being asked to debate a moral, ethical, or aesthetic issue regarding the work. You might be asked to judge a character or group of characters *(Is Caesar responsible for his own demise?)* or the work itself *(Is Jane Eyre a feminist novel?)*. For this kind of essay, there are two important points to keep in mind. First, don't simply base your arguments on your personal feelings and reactions. Every literary essay expects you to read and analyze the work, so search for evidence in the text. What do characters in *1984* have to say about the government of Oceania? What images does Orwell use that might give you a hint about his attitude toward the government? As in any debate, you also need to make sure that you define all the necessary terms before you begin to argue your case. What does it mean to be a "good" society? What makes a novel "feminist"? You should define your terms right up front, in the first paragraph after your introduction.

LITERARY ANALYSIS

Second, remember that strong literary essays make contrary and surprising arguments. Try to think outside the box. In the *1984* example above, it seems like the obvious answer would be no, the totalitarian society depicted in Orwell's novel is *not* good for its citizens. But can you think of any arguments for the opposite side? Even if your final assertion is that the novel depicts a cruel, repressive, and therefore harmful society, acknowledging and responding to the counterargument will strengthen your overall case.

---

5. WRITE THE INTRODUCTION

Your introduction sets up the entire essay. It's where you present your topic and articulate the particular issues and questions you'll be addressing. It's also where you, as the writer, introduce yourself to your readers. A persuasive literary essay immediately establishes its writer as a knowledgeable, authoritative figure.

An introduction can vary in length depending on the overall length of the essay, but in a traditional five-paragraph essay it should be no longer than one paragraph. However long it is, your introduction needs to:

- **Provide any necessary context.** Your introduction should situate the reader and let him or her know what to expect. What book are you discussing? Which characters? What topic will you be addressing?

- **Answer the "So what?" question.** Why is this topic important, and why is your particular position on the topic noteworthy? Ideally, your introduction should pique the reader's interest by suggesting how your argument is surprising or otherwise counterintuitive. Literary essays make unexpected connections and reveal less-than-obvious truths.

- **Present your thesis.** This usually happens at or very near the end of your introduction.

- **Indicate the shape of the essay to come.** Your reader should finish reading your introduction with a good sense of the scope of your essay as well as the path you'll take toward proving your thesis. You don't need to spell out every step, but you do need to suggest the organizational pattern you'll be using.

Your introduction should not:

- **Be vague.** Beware of the two killer words in literary analysis: *interesting* and *important*. Of course, the work, question, or example is interesting and important—that's why you're writing about it!

- **Open with any grandiose assertions.** Many student readers think that beginning their essays with a flamboyant statement, such as "Since the dawn of time, writers have been fascinated by the topic of free will," makes them sound important and commanding. In fact, it sounds pretty amateurish.

- **Wildly praise the work.** Another typical mistake student writers make is extolling the work or author. Your teacher doesn't need to be told that "Shakespeare is perhaps the greatest writer in the English language." You can mention a work's reputation in passing—by referring to *The Adventures of Huckleberry Finn* as "Mark Twain's enduring classic," for example—but don't make a point of bringing it up unless that reputation is key to your argument.

- **Go off-topic.** Keep your introduction streamlined and to the point. Don't feel the need to throw in all kinds of bells and whistles in order to impress your reader—just get to the point as quickly as you can, without skimping on any of the required steps.

---

6. Write the Body Paragraphs

Once you've written your introduction, you'll take the arguments you developed in step 4 and turn them into your body paragraphs. The organization of this middle section of your essay will largely be determined by the argumentative strategy you use, but no matter how you arrange your thoughts, your body paragraphs need to do the following:

- **Begin with a strong topic sentence.** Topic sentences are like signs on a highway: they tell the readers where they are and where they're going. A good topic sentence not only alerts readers to what issue will be discussed in the following paragraphs but also gives them a sense of what argument will be made *about* that issue. "Rumor and gossip play an important role in *The Crucible*" isn't a strong topic sentence because it doesn't tell us very much. "The community's constant gossiping creates an environment that allows false accusations to flourish" is a much stronger topic sentence—

it not only tells us what the paragraph will discuss (gossip) but how the paragraph will discuss the topic (by showing how gossip creates a set of conditions that leads to the play's climactic action).

- **Fully and completely develop a single thought.** Don't skip around in your paragraph or try to stuff in too much material. Body paragraphs are like bricks: each individual one needs to be strong and sturdy or the entire structure will collapse. Make sure you have really proven your point before moving on to the next one.

- **Use transitions effectively.** Good literary essay writers know that each paragraph must be clearly and strongly linked to the material around it. Think of each paragraph as a response to the one that precedes it. Use transition words and phrases such as *however*, *similarly*, *on the contrary*, *therefore*, and *furthermore* to indicate what kind of response you're making.

---

7. WRITE THE CONCLUSION

Just as you used the introduction to ground your readers in the topic before providing your thesis, you'll use the conclusion to quickly summarize the specifics learned thus far and then hint at the broader implications of your topic. A good conclusion will:

- **Do more than simply restate the thesis.** If your thesis argued that *The Catcher in the Rye* can be read as a Christian allegory, don't simply end your essay by saying, "And that is why *The Catcher in the Rye* can be read as a Christian allegory." If you've constructed your arguments well, this kind of statement will just be redundant.

- **Synthesize the arguments rather than summarizing them.** Similarly, don't repeat the details of your body paragraphs in your conclusion. The readers have already read your essay, and chances are it's not so long that they've forgotten all your points by now.

- **Revisit the "So what?" question.** In your introduction, you made a case for why your topic and position are important. You should close your essay with the same sort of gesture. What do your readers know now that they didn't know before? How will that knowledge help them better appreciate or understand the work overall?

- **Move from the specific to the general.** Your essay has most likely treated a very specific element of the work—a single character, a small set of images, or a particular passage. In your conclusion, try to show how this narrow discussion has wider implications for the work overall. If your essay on *To Kill a Mockingbird* focused on the character of Boo Radley, for example, you might want to include a bit in the conclusion about how he fits into the novel's larger message about childhood, innocence, or family life.

- **Stay relevant.** Your conclusion should suggest new directions of thought, but it shouldn't be treated as an opportunity to pad your essay with all the extra, interesting ideas you came up with during your brainstorming sessions but couldn't fit into the essay proper. Don't attempt to stuff in unrelated queries or too many abstract thoughts.

- **Avoid making overblown closing statements.** A conclusion should open up your highly specific, focused discussion, but it should do so without drawing a sweeping lesson about life or human nature. Making such observations may be part of the point of reading, but it's almost always a mistake in essays, where these observations tend to sound overly dramatic or simply silly.

A+ Essay Checklist

Congratulations! If you've followed all the steps we've outlined, you should have a solid literary essay to show for all your efforts. What if you've got your sights set on an A+? To write the kind of superlative essay that will be rewarded with a perfect grade, keep the following rubric in mind. These are the qualities that teachers expect to see in a truly A+ essay. How does yours stack up?

- ✓ Demonstrates a thorough understanding of the book
- ✓ Presents an original, compelling argument
- ✓ Thoughtfully analyzes the text's formal elements
- ✓ Uses appropriate and insightful examples
- ✓ Structures ideas in a logical and progressive order
- ✓ Demonstrates a mastery of sentence construction, transitions, grammar, spelling, and word choice

Suggested Essay Topics

1. What is the significance of Ruth finally learning Precious Auntie's real name?

2. The novel features three generations of women raised by single parents. What traits do the children of single parents display in The Bonesetter's Daughter, and why are these traits significant?

3. How does the idea that Ruth is able to communicate with the spirit of Precious Auntie affect the power dynamic in her relationship with LuLing?

4. How does the relationship between Ruth and Art change over the course of the novel?

5. Are Ruth and Art justified in using deception to get LuLing to move into the assisted living facility?

6. How are the non-Chinese characters in the novel contrasted with the Chinese and Chinese-American characters?

7. Why are LuLing and Mr. Tang able to have a happy relationship together?

GLOSSARY OF LITERARY TERMS

ANTAGONIST

The entity that acts to frustrate the goals of the *protagonist*. The antagonist is usually another *character* but may also be a nonhuman force.

ANTIHERO / ANTIHEROINE

A *protagonist* who is not admirable or who challenges notions of what should be considered admirable.

CHARACTER

A person, animal, or any other thing with a personality that appears in a *narrative*.

CLIMAX

The moment of greatest intensity in a text or the major turning point in the *plot*.

CONFLICT

The central struggle that moves the *plot* forward. The conflict can be the *protagonist*'s struggle against fate, nature, society, or another person.

FIRST-PERSON POINT OF VIEW

A literary style in which the *narrator* tells the story from his or her own *point of view* and refers to himself or herself as "I." The narrator may be an active participant in the story or just an observer.

HERO / HEROINE

The principal *character* in a literary work or *narrative*.

IMAGERY

Language that brings to mind sense-impressions, representing things that can be seen, smelled, heard, tasted, or touched.

MOTIF

A recurring idea, structure, contrast, or device that develops or informs the major *themes* of a work of literature.

NARRATIVE

A story.

LITERARY ANALYSIS

NARRATOR
> The person (sometimes a *character*) who tells a story; the *voice* assumed by the writer. The narrator and the author of the work of literature are not the same thing.

PLOT
> The arrangement of the events in a story, including the sequence in which they are told, the relative emphasis they are given, and the causal connections between events.

POINT OF VIEW
> The *perspective* that a *narrative* takes toward the events it describes.

PROTAGONIST
> The main *character* around whom the story revolves.

SETTING
> The location of a *narrative* in time and space. Setting creates mood or atmosphere.

SUBPLOT
> A secondary *plot* that is of less importance to the overall story but that may serve as a point of contrast or comparison to the main plot.

SYMBOL
> An object, *character*, figure, or color that is used to represent an abstract idea or concept.

SYNTAX
> The way the words in a piece of writing are put together to form lines, phrases, or clauses; the basic structure of a piece of writing.

THEME
> A fundamental and universal idea explored in a literary work.

TONE
> The author's attitude toward the subject or *characters* of a story or poem or toward the reader.

VOICE
> An author's individual way of using language to reflect his or her own personality and attitudes. An author communicates voice through *tone*, *diction*, and *syntax*.

LITERARY ANALYSIS

A NOTE ON PLAGIARISM

Plagiarism—presenting someone else's work as your own—rears its ugly head in many forms. Many students know that copying text without citing it is unacceptable. But some don't realize that even if you're not quoting directly, but instead are paraphrasing or summarizing, it is plagiarism unless you cite the source.

Here are the most common forms of plagiarism:

- Using an author's phrases, sentences, or paragraphs without citing the source

- Paraphrasing an author's ideas without citing the source

- Passing off another student's work as your own

How do you steer clear of plagiarism? You should always acknowledge all words and ideas that aren't your own by using quotation marks around verbatim text or citations like footnotes and endnotes to note another writer's ideas. For more information on how to give credit when credit is due, ask your teacher for guidance or visit www.sparknotes.com.

LITERARY ANALYSIS

Review & Resources

Quiz

1. How did Precious Auntie acquire her scars?

   A. From being attacked by a dog
   B. From being burned by acid
   C. From being attacked with a knife
   D. From boiling ink

2. What happens to Ruth every year around her anniversary?

   A. She suffers fainting spells
   B. She loses the ability to speak
   C. Her hair falls out
   D. She suffers from ringing in her ears

3. What is the name of Ruth's best friend?

   A. Winnie
   B. Wanda
   C. Gwen
   D. Wendy

4. Where does Ruth meet Art?

   A. In a yoga class
   B. In a cooking class
   C. In a bookstore
   D. At a concert

5. What was Edwin Young's profession when he died?

   A. Law student
   B. Accountant
   C. Medical student
   D. Grocer

THE BONESETTER'S DAUGHTER   79

6. How does Ruth break her arm as a child?

    A. An accident on a slide
    B. Falling out of her bedroom window
    C. Getting into a fight after another child insults her mother
    D. Falling down the stairs after her mother pushes her

7. What piece of jewelry does LuLing treasure as a gift from
    her daughter?

    A. A jade ring
    B. A diamond tennis bracelet
    C. Amethyst earrings
    D. A pearl necklace

8. As a young girl, what does Ruth mistakenly end up believing
    about Lance?

    A. That Lance has gotten her pregnant
    B. That Lance is in love with her mother
    C. That Lance is actually her father
    D. That Lance is very rich and is going to adopt her

9. How does LuLing attempt to kill herself when Ruth
    is a teenager?

    A. By swallowing sleeping pills
    B. By hanging herself
    C. By throwing herself out of a window
    D. By stepping into a busy road

10. What nickname does Precious Auntie use for LuLing as a child?

    A. Doggie
    B. Pigeon
    C. Cabbage
    D. Kitten

11. What is the traditional occupation of the Liu family?

    A. Coffin making and carpentry
    B. Wine making
    C. Bonesetting
    D. Ink making

12.   How does Baby Uncle die?

    A.   He is kicked by a horse
    B.   He is shot
    C.   He dies in a fire
    D.   He falls sick with a fever

13.   What conflict between LuLing and Precious Auntie leads to Precious Auntie's suicide?

    A.   LuLing's desire to keep her illegitimate child
    B.   LuLing's desire to marry into the Chang family
    C.   LuLing's desire to emigrate
    D.   LuLing's desire to go to school and study English

14.   Who is GaoLing's first husband?

    A.   A son from the Chang family
    B.   An American geologist
    C.   A well-known scholar and calligrapher
    D.   The owner of a shop that sells paintings and art

15.   How does Kai Jing die?

    A.   He is killed by Japanese soldiers
    B.   He falls ill with malaria
    C.   He dies rescuing LuLing from a fire
    D.   He starves to death

16.   When does LuLing move to Hong Kong?

    A.   When GaoLing departs for America
    B.   When her first husband dies
    C.   When she finds out that she is pregnant
    D.   When she sells the jewels her mother gave her

17.   What is the name of the village where LuLing grew up?

    A.   Blessed Maiden
    B.   Immortal Heart
    C.   Valley of Bones
    D.   Valley of Dogs

18.   What is the name of the assisted living home that LuLing
      moves into?

      A.   Mira Mar Manor
      B.   Avalon Hills
      C.   Immortal Heart Manor
      D.   Precious Place

19.   Who is Ruth named after?

      A.   A teacher at the orphanage where LuLing studied
      B.   An Englishwoman who employed LuLing in
           Hong Kong
      C.   An American actress who LuLing thought was very
           glamorous and beautiful
      D.   The American missionary who sponsored her to
           immigrate

20.   What is the name of the man who translates LuLing's life
      story for Ruth?

      A.   Mr. Young
      B.   Mr. Tang
      C.   Mr. Chang
      D.   Mr. Ping

21.   How many children does Art have?

      A.   One daughter and two sons
      B.   Four sons
      C.   Two daughters
      D.   One son and one daughter

22.   What unexpected change occurs after LuLing moves into
      the assisted living home?

      A.   She begins to volunteer in the local community
      B.   She begins a relationship with the man who translated
           her life story
      C.   She begins to study music
      D.   She becomes interested in spending time with Art's
           children

REVIEW & RESOURCES

23. What is the family name of LuLing's mother?

     A.   Gu
     B.   Wu
     C.   Tang
     D.   Liu

24. How does Art and Ruth's relationship change by the end of
     the novel?

     A.   They decide to get married
     B.   They decide to separate
     C.   They decide to stay in a relationship but live apart so
           that Ruth can have more independence
     D.   They decide to have an open relationship

25. Who finally confirms Precious Auntie's name for Ruth?

     A.   Uncle Edwin
     B.   The man who translates LuLing's life story
     C.   LuLing
     D.   GaoLing

SUGGESTIONS FOR FURTHER READING

Adams, Bella. *Amy Tan*. Manchester: Manchester University Press, 2005.

Ho, Wendy. *In Her Mother's House: The Politics of Asian-American Mother Daughter Writing*. Walnut Creek: Altamira Press, 1999.

Huntley, E. D. *Amy Tan: A Critical Companion*. Westport: Greenwood Press, 1998.

Lanpo, Jia. *The Story of Peking Man: From Archaeology to Mystery*. Oxford: Oxford University Press, 1990.

Snodgrass, Mary Ellen. *Amy Tan: A Literary Companion*. New York: McFarland, 2004.

Tan, Amy. *Where the Past Begins: A Writer's Memoir*. New York: Harper Collins, 2017.

NOTES

NOTES

NOTES

NOTES

NOTES

NOTES

NOTES

NOTES

Notes